Bellum Locket

R. E. Chisholme

First published in 2012 by
The Irregular Special Press
for Baker Street Studios Ltd
Endeavour House
170 Woodland Road, Sawston
Cambridge, CB22 3DX, UK

ISBN: 1-901091-54-6 (10 digit)
ISBN: 978-1-901091-54-0 (13 digit)

Cover Concept & Illustration: IrregularCharlie (Charlie Dix)

Typeset in 8/11/20pt Palatino

About the Author

I was born in 1998 in Wales. Being partly Welsh has influenced more in my life than one would think. I know people who don't really care about where they were born, but having a love for the Welsh countryside has really made me care. A few times a year I would visit there, and as I grew this became more and more. As a child, the five hour trips seemed tedious (and being furiously car sick didn't help), so I didn't go as much then as I do now.

My parents split when I was only six, but it didn't hit me as bad as you would think. I didn't really understand it then, which made the blow easier to take as I just grew up with it. I don't mind it now, twice the Christmas presents and two different houses with two completely different atmospheres! This sounds pretty good to me.

Growing up, I found myself writing small stories and imagining lots of things, my games as a child were entertaining and complicated. I always hated how when we grow we lose that ability to get lost in our imagination outside our minds. I still use my imagination to imagine different things, especially with stories or my book.

Now, when I first started writing my book, it was actually just a story I thought I'd write. I attempted a book only a month before and although I got to twenty-six pages, I deleted it. It didn't feel right because I didn't like the story line.

People always ask me "What inspired you to start writing?" Well, I needed a way out. My family had been through some troubles and there seemed to be only a pen waiting for me, the only thing that would listen, so I just began to write.

My book was interesting to me, but back then it was only a personal project, so I forgot about it for a few months. In those few months tough times erupted, but I suppose it made it better for when I began writing again.

I thought about it often as the New Year began, and I decided to have a look at it, see if I wanted it anymore. But as I read through, I began writing again, and then it became a project.

Once it hit fifty pages my family started taking a light interest, asking me how it was going and what I was writing about. I never thought I'd write as much as I did, but then as I started hitting ninety pages and more, my family and friends were telling me not to give up on it, so I didn't. I'll admit I had moments where I really just wanted to throw it all in the bin because I was annoyed, but I didn't. My Nan was the key to make me keep doing it, she was the first person to read it all and she is still the first person to read anything fresh and new I write.

I hope you enjoy the book, reader.

Becca

Preface

My Fellow Reader,

Throughout my younger childhood years, I was constantly writing stories. These were the classic sort of childrens' ideas, dragons, flight and heroes. My stories, despite their classic ways, always had a dark aspect. They always seemed to be shaped by something unfair, or wrong. Writing was, and is, my way of expressing myself and the world we live.

I often view my pen as my sword, the paper as my shield because to me, that is what they are. Books take you out of your shoes and into an entirely different world, and that is why I enjoyed writing my book the most. It was a break for me. I hope readers feel the same, and they escape from sometimes a harsh reality and into an entirely different one.

Books and writing both have helped me through tough stages in my life. At midnight when a nightmare awoke me, a book was always there, or a pen and paper. I often found dreams scared me as a child. Now, at the beginning of my teenage years, I have learnt to prepare myself; I even control some of my nightmares and turn them into normal, nice dreams.

Through writing I have learnt many things, how people work, how things change ... but mostly, I have learnt to recognise that there are two sides to every story.

Enjoy.

Becca

For you,
For family, for friends, for loyalty.

Chapter One

The Return

$\mathcal{S}$he ran. Her heart pounded, her feet ached, but she ran with all her heart, because this was all she could do. Whoever was following her seemed to have stopped, or hid, because when she finally gave into her aching feet, and turned; she saw no one. Maybe that's it, she thought.

Maybe they won't ever try and catch me again ... She spoke too soon.

Someone stepped out from behind an oak tree, they were so far away, and she wasn't able to see the rifle in his hand or the ammunition in his belt, or the smile on his face. But, she did sense, the danger, ready to shoot, hidden in his rifle. She could sense it in the air. And before he had the chance to shoot her, she ran again.

The wind was starting to pick up, causing her hair to whip around her face and block her eyesight, she tried to brush it out of her eyes desperately, the book slipped from her grip and as she did so, it fell on the floor. She stopped, ran towards the book and picked it up, but now, as she looked round, they were coming fast, they were close, she needed a way out; before they caught up.

She searched her book, flipping through the pages while running ... she had no trouble reading the words; it was finding the right page that was the problem.

At last, she found it, a blank page.

She seized the page with her hand and pressed on it as hard as she could. She felt a huge beam fall over her, and just before she dissolved into safety, she looked around her.

The dead trees, dead grass, dead animals lying on what Elisia could only describe as hard rock with lines on it ... She didn't know what was going on, and frankly, she didn't want to. Ever since she'd arrived here one year ago, she'd seen people die; animals hunted and sensed more danger and fear than ever before.

The man had stopped; he lowered his strange wand ... He was looking at the light, as if he'd never seen anything like it. She knew he was lying (although she couldn't sense it), the force of the spells that they drop from the sky everyday was good enough evidence that he was lying. They did magic ... she knew they did.

Elisia grabbed her chance, she cast a spell over him; it was the only one she promised herself she would never use, unless they deserved it. She took out her wand, pointed at him, and said: "Veritas et mendacium ..."

Her wand let off a puff of mist, which crawled over the floor until it reached him. Then the mist climbed up his legs and stomach until it reached his head, then, the man, not knowing or seeing the mist, breathed it all in.

And that was the last thing Elisia saw.

She dissolved into the witch telegraphing point, where witches everywhere jumped into long tubes that reached towards the ceiling and further. All of them had an 'upwards' spell upon them; making every single witch fly upwards into the world they wanted to be in. Every witch knew which one went where, and you had to be careful, in case you went to the wrong place, where they were at war or something.

But supposing you weren't very good at remembering things, each one was colour coded, making every sparkling white, floor tile and wall tile, shine with proudest of all glories of every colour of the rainbow.

Elisia took her blessings and held her book tight, not to anyone's surprise, they were all carrying books. No matter where they came from, it was one of the ways they could interact with their goddess, Selphina. She was the first ever witch to live, she made all the clan names, the buildings, everything. The books we're not only for that, they had each day written in them, but only till one last page was blank, then the first lot was wiped out, and it started all over again. Witches knew nothing of the uses of being cowardly or having memories, they only worked upon courage, defence and being intelligent.

Elisia, who's first thought was; on what the weather was like in Arroondera (her world); took a look at the purple tube she needed to step into. She saw clouds, dark ones at that. Least it wasn't raining, she thought.

Knowing what to do now was no trouble at all; she took her book with her hand, and tapped it once. It vanished with a puff of smoke, and she jumped into the tube.

The best thing about the tube was, you didn't go too slow or too fast; you went just right. It takes ten minutes to get to Arroondera, so Elisia thought of what she was going to say to her clan queen, Kerkavia.

She decided it was best to say she was sorry, although she didn't see what she was sorry for ... after ten long pondering minutes, she arrived, hovering, in the middle of the town square.

The witch floated down and waited until the charm was gone; testing every few moments to see if she jumped normally, or hovered then hit the ground.

After it was gone, she looked around.

The town was full of brick white paths leading in four directions. One went east, others south, west and north. They went past many witch houses, wand shops and clothes shops. Even, demon clothes shops, but this was only for spies, so it was only open at twilight. However, out of all these amazing and incredible shops, the one that interested Elisia most was the unusual items shop.

She liked the idea of mystery and ways to defeat dark magic. Obviously, not all witches are good, some kill others, some hurt others, some even bury others alive, however, that's only when wars begin ... usually.

Elisia looked at herself in one of the shop windows, her reflection showed that the long black plait, that she had took so long to complete, had come undone. Her piercing green eyes had become reddened from tiredness, and her clothes were torn. Her lips were chapped and bleeding; her face was surprisingly clean, apart from the odd dirt mark ...

But before she could take in more of the fresh air and beautiful houses, even take another step forwards, she saw Kerkavia, rushing towards her.

"Elisia! Elisia! Thank goodness! Selphina told me you were coming! I was worried!"

Elisia turned to look this woman in the face before she spoke.

Kerkavia was beautiful, she had long blue silky hair and a carefully cut fringe. She was thin, but her arms and legs showed muscle. She seemed to float. She was two hundred and twenty-four years old, but that counted as young in witch years.

"Follow me; we have much to catch up on."

Elisia followed; it wasn't as if she had much choice.

Kerkavia took Elisia into her palace, everything shined, and everything had a value to it, which was bad. Elisia was good at breaking things.

Chapter Two

The Wicked and the Wise

Kerkavia opened the biggest oak doors in the whole palace, Elisia watched as this magnificent room was revealed. The oak floor was shining as if it was wet, and as Elisia looked more around the room, she saw a few broomsticks washing the floor all by themselves; with a bucket following in the broomsticks wake.

To Elisia's amazement there was only one table set out with two chairs.

"Are you hungry, Elisia?" Kerkavia said, as she walked into the hall.

Elisia knew that it was useless to lie to a witch; they can sense betrayal, sickness, secrecy, hunger and distress.

Elisia was about to reply when Kerkavia yelled at one of the broomsticks. It froze in its position and then carried on the way it was working.

"Stupid things, they have a mind of their own sometimes … anyway, as I said, are you hungry?"

Elisia stood and gazed for a little while at the broomstick, and as if it knew, it swished itself right behind the table and chairs, out of her sight.

"Yes, but I will have something when I return home."

Kerkavia nodded, and then beckoned Elisia to follow her. "Mind your step, the broom sticks might 'accidently' smack you if you dirt up the floor, best to try and please them."

Kerkavia took her down several halls, in rooms, through more doors then the young witch could count without losing track, and finally a plain old white door. To be honest, she didn't think much was behind it. But Kerkavia opened it with a key and pulled Elisia through.

Five minutes later and they were sitting on cushions by a fire, the floor was wooden and had a dark red carpet on it, and the walls were red with white stripes. The windows stood behind them both, showering them in light. Elisia didn't like it, but she didn't say anything.

Kerkavia tapped the floor, and suddenly a tea set on a silver tray popped up there.

"Take one if you want one, I think you can make it yourself now." She said smiling.

"Now, Elisia, I know some of how you came into the Demon World, I know you fell out of this one."

To any non-magical being, this would have been more of a cartoon strip then a serious matter. Here, though, witches take matters very seriously, and this made Elisia nervous.

"But, Elisia, forgive my rudeness, you could have only fallen, and survived, by knowing you were being pushed. Do not lie to me dear child, because you know I shall know if you lie. I have many Wand Spies, they watch out for you, report to me through their wands. And none of them saw you fall ..."

She couldn't help it; she dug her finger nails into her hand.

"Except one, they did see it! He said someone, had pushed you. Now, I do not expect you to tell me, but there is no spell to stop any witch from falling a great height."

Kerkavia waited for Elisia to answer, and when no reply came, she sighed.

"I expect that you are unwilling to tell me, it is, rather embarrassing going into the Demon world. Crazy and sinful souls live there, but we must live above them, we have no choice. It is where dear Selphina placed us."

Elisia already knew this, it was if Kerkavia didn't care that it was an on-going tradition for a witch's mum to tell their daughters these things, and to teach them magic. But she caught herself just in time, no witch ever shouts at a Clan

Witch. Yes, witches may shout to others or at others, but it was only respectful to talk to a Clan Witch politely.

Kerkavia frowned.

"Elisia this is a full witch trial, if you don't tell me right here, right now, you'll have to say it out there ..."

Kerkavia sighed again.

"My wand spy will be speaking, only the one that saw you of course, but you won't be able to see him, he is a Demon Spy ... I dearly hope you understand why you cannot see him. But do not panic, they are only interested in how you managed to get to the Demon World, he will talk of nothing else."

"Please, follow me into the grand hall, and then I will call them in."

Kerkavia stood up, walked over to the door and opened it. Elisia felt as if someone had just released all the air from her lungs, breathing deeply, she walked through into another hallway.

The Clan Witch led the poor child, again, through many hallways; rooms ... doors, until finally they were back where they had started. The brooms had gone now, the floor was dry, and there were only two tables and one of the tables only had one chair! (Elisia thought this was a bit small considering it's a 'full' witch case. Who will sit there?) .

It was only when Elisia sat by Kerkavia that she realized she knew about the witch courts. She couldn't sit by the side of friends, she had to sit on the small table, and away from everyone she knew and trusted.

Soon, the hall was full of entering witches, some from other clans and worlds, others from different universes altogether. This made Elisia gulp, she knew what had happened to her was rare, but she didn't know how rare it was; until now.

She watched as every witch created a chair, and sat upon it, even the Spies did so. They weren't placed by the table, neither we're the witches, they made a circle around it, some even told off others for going to close to Elisia, as if she had some kind of deadly disease.

15

But it was only when they told her to sit on a small table, alone, on a stage, did she feel more lonely and unique than ever. Her mother had told her that uniqueness was something to be proud of, something to own and cherish, but her mother wasn't here now, and her father was long gone.

She pinched herself hard on the hand, she couldn't think about that now, not when she had a story to tell.

Suddenly all the voices died away, then a man with a long black beard and pointed hat, stood up.

"Are you Elisia Ivy Crewman?" He said. His voice was gruff and low, but it echoed through the hall.

"Yes." Her voice was small and a whisper.

"Please speak louder child!"

"Yes." Her voice was louder this time.

"And are you the only witch under one hundred and sixty to enter the Demon World?"

"Yes, well, that I know of ..."

She was relaxed this time, because Kerkavia nodded at her, as if to say 'relax, stay focused and listen. Tell the truth'.

"In the month of February, day twelve, year four thousand and thirty-six, did you accidently fall into the Demon World?"

"Yes."

"Please, I ask you to tell all of us what happened on that day. Take your time, and the audience may question."

Chapter Three

Alone

*E*lisia cast her eyes around the hall full of eyes, eyes that were staring at her, eyes that wanted answers that maybe even Elisia did not have ...

Her nerves started to get the better of her, she shook lightly, although inside she knew she was shaking violently as if ill. Her heart was pumping blood fast, perhaps too fast. She was frightened, scared of telling so many judgmental eyes her dark story ...

What did she fear? Laughing?

No, Elisia did not fear the laughing. There would be none.

She feared the concern.

She looked down at the table, took a deep, shaking breath, and began.

"I woke up, and as usual I had the intentions of travelling to the dining hall. I was walking along when suddenly I felt a little dizzy, I guessed it was from hunger or something ... but I kept walking. I went down the little alley and through the hill, but that's when things, went a bit ... funny ..."

A woman in the audience stood up.

"In what way was it funny?"

"Well, it went a little odd. I remember seeing someone, so I ran up to them to ask them what time it was, but they asked me to "Leave them alone" I guessed it was a spy, so I kept on walking. I got distracted wondering what the time was, so I wondered whether I ought to go back and check, but I knew there were other ways of checking the time." This seemed to satisfy her, she sat down again.

"I knew that you could sometimes tell the time by looking at the Demon World, so I went right to the edge of the valley. It wasn't far to walk ..."

Elisia was interrupted by a cough behind her, "Excuse me? Miss Crewman? I'll take it from here."

Elisia knew it was the spy, he was invisible, but she could sense that he was young and from Crowdannya, she heard it in his accent. Nobody asked who he was, but he told them he was 'the' spy, and then carried on.

"I saw her, crouchin' down, tryin' to get a little look at the Demon Time, when I heard a runnin' man. I turned towards the sound but nothin' was there, and when I turned back, she was gone. I drew out my wand, but they fired at me. I was immobile, and when I managed to get back on my feet, they were long gone. I tried to call out for this girl, but she weren't respondin', I called for Kerkavia straightaway." He gestured towards her.

"Kerkavia and I then went back for help, but there was nothin' we could do. The demon world ain't no friend to us as we all know, so we just had to hope and pray she survived. Here she is. Safe and sound."

Elisia looked up at him in shock. In his voice she had felt the bitter taste of anger, not from sensing, but from natural common sense. He seemed to have been talking with his jaw clenched shut.

He caught her eye and gave her a smile and a respectful nod; never mind then.

The old man slowly stood up shakily, you had to praise him for even attempting to stand up.

"This investigation shall be talked through by the council, if Miss Kerkavia would please join us." He spoke loudly and in a hoarse way, and a bit shakily.

"Yes, I would most gladly." Kerkavia frowned at the spy, and Elisia knew why, they both sensed secrecy within his words. She looked at Elisia as if to say 'find out'.

The hall was full of voices again, and this made Elisia gasp with relief.

"You were nervous then were ya, Miss Crewman?" This voice came from the air.

"I thought spies weren't allowed to talk to witches?"

"I am, because I saved your life basically."

"Oh, well I was ... what are you not telling the witches? You've got a secret, haven't you?"
There was a delicate pause.

"No! What are you on about, child?" He laughed, "I've got nothin' to hide!"

She dimly saw the spy walk away; she sat back comfortably in her seat. Now that she thought about it, she realized that confronting him straight off wasn't the best idea, especially when he had things to hide. Elisia slapped her head in frustration for her stupidity.

"I really need to start being more ..."

Her words drifted off as she spotted an invisible shape speedily heading towards her, rising from her seat and stepping out from behind the cover of the table, she went to confront the spy.

"Come back to tell the truth then?" She stopped walking.

He was still coming; fast.

"I appreciate your excitement to see me, but seriously, slow down. We don't want you to hurt yourself, now do we?" She joked, hoping to hide her concern. Was he about to attack her? Was he annoyed because she had outwitted his plans and revealed a secret or something?

He was close to her; and he wasn't stopping.

He didn't even look right, this spy seemed to have completely change shape since the last time she saw him ... and he seemed to be reaching out for her with red claws she could only dimly see, targeting her, like she was his prey. She whispered to herself, suddenly panicking.

She was within arm's reach.

Elisia turned to run; too late.

She felt a cold hand clasp her wrist in a tight embrace that even Elisia knew she could not get out of. She began to feel increasingly weakened, like part of her was being drained out. Elisia began to collapse on to the floor, knees buckling; she stared at her arms as the skin on them slowly began stretching over her bones. She felt sick; she had to release this creature's grip.

She slowly looked around as witches began running towards her, obviously they had realized she was in danger, sensed it in the air around her.

Her eyes stared at a cloaked figure standing in the doorway. It shot a spell at the creature, sending it flying back on to the hard marble floor, and setting Elisia's arm free.

The young witch scrambled up, hardly noticing that her skin was slowly going back to its usual state, that the part of her that was drained was flooding back and making her finger tips tingle.

She drew her wand at the thing, determined to make it pay for what it had done.

She shakily asked one of the witches what the creature was, but a dim figure standing next to her gave her the answer she wanted.

"It's a vampire Elisia ..."

A dark silence hung itself over the hall.

Elisia tried to calm her nerves, but she was shaking no matter what she did. In the Demon World, vampires were no more than a myth, but in any witch land, they existed. They didn't suck out your blood, they sucked out magic, but getting it used against them was fatal. A few years ago a witch had managed to stumble back to her world with little magic left, Elisia was only young when she had seen the witch, but she still remembers how the witch was practically only skin and bone. Elisia shivered, staring at her now back to normal arms. Vampires took refuge in dark places, this one really had to have been hungry to come out in daylight.

"What do we do with it?"

"Should we kill it?"

"Nah, that's cruel, we should let it back out into the wild."

"Pah! So it can kill more people! I say we kill it!"

Elisia saw the spy shake his head as the witches uproar began to get more fierce, more and more vicious things were said to do with the vampire.

"Just open the windows." He yelled over the uproar.

The witches clicked their fingers reluctantly; clearly disappointed they couldn't make a meal out of the creature (which was actually one of the more vicious suggestions). All the windows opened and the vampire became visible.

Its skin was as brick white, its eyes were black. Its mouth did not have fangs like demon myth, but holes in its cheeks, making it easier for it to breathe in magic.

Elisia watched it, as the cold air leaked in, it started to fade, and with a high-pitched scream, it vanished … leaving the echo of its scream behind, and leaving Elisia, shook up; fearful for her safety.

*****

"Are you alright there, Miss Crewman?" The spy said quietly, leading her to her seat.

"A little shaken, but I'm fine." Elisia said back, hoping to give a winning convincing smile. It clearly was not.

"No you're not." He made her sit down on the table. "Stay here, I'm goin' to tell your Clan Witch."

"Wait!" She said, reaching out her hand as if to stop him, "Is there something I can call you by?"

"I'll ask your Clan Witch."

She just saw the outline of him walk away.

Elisia sat alone; trying to not let her brain run away with the idea of 'what if the vampire had killed her?'. She cast her mind back to the moment just before almost dying; there had been a cloaked figure by the door. Who was that? Why had they saved her?

She continued asking herself these questions while staring at the door for two main reasons. One, it calmed her. Two, it stopped her thinking about death.

After a while, she was calm. Her heart was beating normally, but by then the pain in her head really started kicking in (another side effect from nearly being devoured by a vampire), she couldn't just sit here contemplating death, cloaked figures and what not. So, with that, she got up and wondered into the sea of standing witches.

"Excuse me?" Elisia said to a kind looking witch, "Do you know where the Clan Witch, Zedaina, is? I need to speak to her."

"Oh, yes, she's just over there sweetie." The witch pointed to another witch wearing a dark blue dress. Elisia praised her own skills for being judgmental on appearances; she seemed to have a talent for picking honest kind people to talk to. Elisia approached Zedaina, she realized that she had dark blue eyes too. They called her 'Witch of Wisdom' and Elisia could see why.

"Zedaina Wisdom, I come to you with many questions." The young witch curtsied.

Elisia knew this sounded posh and unlike her, but she had been told this was the way to greet a Clan Witch from another world. It was polite. Elisia wanted information from this witch, and witches were unlikely to talk to you if you were just plain rude. It was common logic.

"Ah, dear child, you may go on. Excuse me sisters, I must talk to the child."

Elisia tried not to feel irritated that someone had just called her a child yet again, and followed Zedaina.

Zedaina slowly walked over to a table, Elisia really had to applaud the woman on the posture she had. You could put books on that witch's head and they would stay still. Elisia sat down carefully after Zedaina, minding her dress.

"Zedaina, I feel in danger, I have been told by many great ones that you have taught people to see things others cannot, can you teach me?" Elisia begun, getting straight to the matter.

"Ah, well child, you must understand that many have come and asked me the same question. So I will give you the same answer I gave them. If you seek a great mind, and the sight to see all, you must learn the art of Trust and Living."

And with that, Zedaina got up and walked off, leaving Elisia highly confused. Trust and Living?

Well, Elisia trusts and she breathes … clearly she's got that art mastered and sorted.

Suddenly a voice came from the air.

"I'm back; your Clan Witch said you must call me Spy. Until such time when I quit, then you can know my name."

"So is she coming?" She said, getting up.

"Oh yes, she's comin' now, you might want to take your seat again."

Elisia nodded and slowly walked over to the table with a small feeling of dread beginning to grow; this feeling seemed to bubble over as she took her seat. This time she sat down with caution. Just in case something else was ready to try and smack her to death, or take her hostage, or something.

Soon, the council started filling in, taking away her worry of safety because of the surrounding people and replacing it with a worry of the verdict. A different man stood up. He was tall, but old.

"Elisia Crewman, you must report to magic lessons here, in this room at a certain time. We think you have more magic than you can handle, and this will help you control it. You will get lessons from the Universal Spiritess, who is here now to talk to you."

Elisia felt a voice inside her say "lessons? Can't handle?" and "how an earth did they get that from being pushed off a flipping big cliff!"

A person, no not a person, a spiritual woman, stood up from the table. Her hair flowed outwards a little bit and each beautiful strand was the colour of a peach; she was pale, she looked as fragile as a feather. Her friendly smile echoed through the hall. She literally floated as well, but what didn't amaze Elisia was the fact her eyes glittered like the stars at night, or the fact she was faded a little; the one thing that did amaze Elisia was the fact she could instantly smell despair. Spiritesses had become so because they had their heart broken, but wizened from it. Learned from their mistakes, helped others, the whole lot. She was created, piece by piece, from the balance of the sinful and surprising universe.

"My name is Poppy, please don't get up!" She giggled (Elisia wondered why this annoyed her so much), "I'm named after the flower I created; I'm not allowed to tell any witch my last name, forgive me! This rare happening has made me wonder in delight and confusion, I looked around the whole universe, gathering information, but I could not find the answer, so I set out looking for Elisia myself. You witches are skilled; I was most impressed when I came here. Happiness of seeing you filled my soul gratefully.

"I shall explain myself, for all them spies and witches who have never heard of a Spiritess. A Spiritess has the universe in their souls; they know everything, the past, present, and future.

"I can see what you're feeling and how many heart breaks you have had, I can see you, as yourself, even when you're acting. I can channel into your minds thoughts, and listen to calls you may not even make, but your heart does." She gestured to everyone in the hall.

"We have healing powers, but certain things cannot be healed. We can explore thoughout your memories and help you overcome fears. We have fort …"

Elisia didn't see how this was helping, most witches knew about spiritesses, even the spies did. Surely she would know that.

But actually, she would know. So why was she saying all this?

Elisia cast her eyes around the hall; she saw that every single witch seemed to be looking around in confusion too. Some were even whispering to each other.

"Hey, Elisia, do you know why she's sayin' this?"

This whisper came from the air.

"I don't know, hey, can she see you?"

"No, not if I blank my mind out."

Elisia was shocked at this revelation for a minute, "You can blank your mind out?" She asked going off topic.

"Yes, takes trainin' for a few years, why?"

"Can you see who she's aiming this at?"

She saw the spy dimly nod, and then he totally disappeared.

Elisia kept trying to see where he was, sometimes she saw him dimly, but that was only when he forgot to block his mind out. Sometimes she couldn't see him at all; she even whispered out his name once or twice to check he was there.

After a while she adapted herself to keep an eye on the Spiritess, but it didn't seem to mind that someone was spying on it, so Elisia looked at her clan witch instead, and found she instantly sensed despair.

Her senses came alert instantly; she sat up straight and grasped her wand. She felt it become alert as well.

Something tapped her on the shoulder, making her almost turn around and shoot a spell.

"Hey, calm down. Why yaw all stressed out?"

"I can sense despair …"

"Who's feelin' despair? Who's the source?"

"My Clan Witch, spy on her."

And when Elisia realized how rude she was being, she then added, "… please …"

She heard the spy give a little chuckle of laughter, then he went silent and she couldn't see him anymore.

After half an hour, he returned. He said he couldn't find a single reason why she would be feeling like that.

"Are you sure?"

"Positive."

At this point, she was getting bored. People were still rambling on and asking questions about things Elisia didn't understand now, at the present time.

Her senses by this time were slowing, she was tired, but every time she tried to fall asleep the spy woke her up, telling her it would look rude.

"So what shall we do about the child's wand?"

Elisia sat up so straight, so fast that she felt her arm click, it started to hurt. But she ignored it; she needed to hear this.

"Well," said the Spiritess, "it's only a training wheel, and she's done a lot more spells nowadays, but just to be sure ..."

The Spiritess called up Elisia, and asked Elisia to do a spell without her wand.

Elisia calmed herself, closed her eyes, clicked her fingers and imagined at the same time that a chair was going to appear in front of her.

She heard a pop, and sure enough, when she opened her eyes, a chair was there. It was just how she imagined it, brown with studded gold buttons.

"Now," said Poppy, "stand over by that wall and call the chair, if it works it will slide and stop in front of you."

Elisia walked over to the plain white wall (why hadn't someone added some sort of pattern?) she didn't dare look around, she was being stared at and she didn't need to look at everyone to confirm it. It didn't bother her much; she was used to being stared at in the demon world, so she naturally ignored them.

She faced the chair and stared, she was imagining it moving, over and over, as if a part of a film was on a replay. She imagined the chair moving swiftly up, hovering, moving carefully, and stopping in front of her.

Suddenly the chair hovered up, and started moving slowly towards her. Sometimes it jolted, but it kept moving.

She kept looking at it, but her focus faded due to everyone talking in surprise, and suddenly the chair moved forwards too fast. She had expected it to stop by now, but it hadn't, it was moving faster and faster across the floor, heading straight for Elisia. (*"Deja vous ..."* Elisia thought.)

"Elisia! You need to move child!"

Elisia already knew this, and stepped aside. The chair crashed into the wall with a tremendous bang, flipped backwards and landed on its back.

Poppy glided forwards and said "This child, is not a rubbish witch Miss Manuel, she is an extremely quick thinker. She moved aside, but waited for it to stop before she moved. We should praise her for being brave."

26

Elisia admitted quietly to herself that she just moved because she wanted, and didn't think anything like that. But, she kept quiet, compliments were always appreciated.

"Now, this child is hungry, you all are tired. If, Kerkavia you would like to stand, I would feel most happy."

Kerkavia scowled at Poppy for ordering her around, then stood up, and addressed the hall. "Please, feel free to leave when you would like sisters. Spies, you will come to my office at nine tonight to receive new orders, now if ..."

Elisia suddenly had an idea.

Chapter Four

Target in Sight

$\mathcal{E}$ ven though Kerkavia told them to leave three times, the witches still had questions, which meant Elisia couldn't leave. Poppy had to step in after a while though; she sensed Elisa's extreme tiredness … or she saw Elisia's eyes droop after an another hour of rambling.

When Elisia finally went outside, she was wide awake; she had one whole hour to tell the one friend she needed to tell her plan too, and that was Axinda.

The fresh air opened up to Elisia, the night time owls croaked to each other from far branches. She was home. Elisia took a deep breath in … and jumped. A giant shriek of happiness from behind her had frightened her. She spun round to greet her fellow best friend, and the way they acted, anyone would have thought they were sisters. Elisia hugged her friend and watched in amusement as she jumped around screaming in happiness; when this began to get boring, Elisia calmed her.

"We've got something we need to do."

"What is it?"

Axinda, who was, sometimes, nicknamed Axe, soon nodded hesitantly in agreement to the idea.

"C'mon, come to the Lignum Tee, we got to move." Elisia whispered.

"Wont we need your mum's spell book?"

"It's already there! C'mon!"

They ran down the brick white path, crawled on all fours as they went past windows, ducked as the trees tried to pull their hair or trip them up, until they came to the biggest tree in the area.

This was the Lignum Tree.

Elisia started to climb first; she grabbed the first branch, climbed up, and then jumped to the second branch. The trick to climbing this giant thing was not to look down. The tree liked Elisia and Axe, so it remained immobile when they were climbing it.

She could have used an upwards spell, or a hover charm, but Elisia had always just climbed this tree; she wanted to keep the tradition going. A memory caught her mind as she touched one of the branches, when she was younger she tried to climb this tree. It had started well, until she slipped and began plummeting to the pathway below. The tree had sprung into action and caught her leg; it had safely lowered her down and patted her head.

Elisia smiled.

Carefully lowering herself down onto the biggest branch, she let her feet dangle as she took out her mother's spell book, a feather, an inkpot and a small red book. It had a broken spine from when the young witch had sat on it as a child.

Axe soon joined her.

"Look," Elisia said, "We only got half hour until we've got to be there, so this is what we'll do."

Elisia drew the conference building with the ink and the feather; she had been in there earlier today, which helped her draw it.

"We'll crouch here." She pointed at the side of the building, just under the window. "We'll be under the spells, and then go up on the roof top. Nah, should we just go by the wall? Yeah, just by the wall will do. Then we can make it see through, so we can see. Also we'll put the …" She flipped through the spell book, "the speak charm on the wall, so we can hear them."

"El, what if we get caught …"

"We won't, we'll be invisible!"

"But the spies can see us, and they surround the building."

Elisia already knew this, but they were all going to be in the building weren't they?

"It's the *Spy* conference; they are not going to be there! Plus, we can blame it on the upward spell, saying that we were experimenting and we didn't realise or something ..."

Axe still didn't look reassured.

"C'mon, I just got back ... please! Please! Please do this Axe!"

Axe still didn't look convinced at all, Elisia knew that given a minute, she would agree.

"Fine, but if I go down I'm taking you with me."

A feeling of relief spread through Elisia's body, thank Witch World that Axinda was so easy to win over. Elisia wouldn't have gone alone.

Axe went down first this time, Elisia needed to put her stuff into the hole again. Carrying her mum's book in her hand, she started to climb down too, but not before she healed a piece of bark that had been cut by rabbits. The tree shook its leaves gratefully.

Gracefully landing down on the floor next to Axe, Elisia placed her mother's spell book on the floor and looked at Axe. Her friend's facial expression said it all, Axe was nervous.

"This won't hurt, I've done it before, so don't worry." Elisia had indeed done this spell before, but only once, when she was sleeping in the Demon world, and had felt in danger of the armed men walking down the road.

Elisia cupped her hands and placed them in front of her mouth, she thought 'invisibility is silence'; 'invisibility is silence', over and over, until she felt a tingle in her mouth. Then, she breathed on her hands and cupped them quickly; the tingling was in her hands now. Slowly, she moved her hands little so they hovered above her friends head, then she opened them.

A dark blue sparkle came out of her hands, it fell until every last one had settled on Axe, with a flash of dark blue light, Axe could no longer be seen.

Elisia repeated this process on herself, and they began to walk down the road.

It was total darkness now; Elisia was starting to feel afraid of the task she had thought of. Yes, she needed to listen, but no way was she as confident as before. She didn't say this to Axe obviously, she knew Axe would instantly pull out of her plan, and if she did that, that was it. Elisia wouldn't go alone.

So, they walked in silence … until they heard a familiar voice.

"No, shut up! We got to be quiet; we aren't supposed to be out. Look, we'll just go to t'is meeting, then leave alri'ht?"

Elisia and Axe froze, they knew that voice. They knew that voice better than anyone else! That was the voice of Harley Marlow, a pig headed pigeon. Every boy had to become a Spy whether they liked it or not (unless they had a skill which made them suitable for a Trained Assassin or a Merchant), but Harley thought he was simply outstanding, and that he would be the first ever 'man' not to be a Spy … or anything else.

Then they heard another voice.

"Harley, we aren't going to get into deep trouble are we? I don't want Clan Queen, as if she's all that, shouting at me."

Elisia almost wanted to smack her, it was Vanessa, and she also thought she was amazing. She was the worst witch, in Elisia's opinion, to ever live. They were brother and sister, and both snot nosed brats.

So many memories of embarrassment were tied to those two. There was one in the breakfast dining hall where Harley had shamed Elisia to the core of her being, another where Vanessa had set Elisia up … over the years of living, the hate for the pair Elisia possessed had grown and swelled to the brink of wanting to hurt them both."

"Axe, we got to move!" Elisia whispered.

"Why?" Axe replied, whispering even quieter.

"She'll sense betrayal."

Elisia knew Axe was looking at her in a way to say, 'oooh no'.

Elisia started at a sprint; she tried to pace herself, so she wouldn't be breathing too loud. Axe, however, wasn't a great runner, and soon Elisia had to slow to let Axe breathe and catch up.

"Don't worry, it's just round the corner, we can walk."

Hearing Axe's sigh of relief, they began to walk toward the castle.

As they walked round the corner, they realised why this would be tricky.

Chapter Five

Jumps and Slides

Axe stood still.

"No. No! Let's go back! We have to go back!!"

Elisia hadn't expected this. She hadn't expected to see them, not here, not in safety. Not guarding the castle.

"Please, Elisia, this is too hard. C'mon, you know what they do, you know what they did. Let's leave." Axe was pulling at her arm, whining.

"No." She replied stubbornly.

"Elisia, I can feel them from here."

"Were going in, they can't see us."

"No Elisia. Look at them! Do you remember what they are? Remember what they did to Jimmy? When he tried to put a spell on one?"

Elisia remembered. Two years back, Jimmy Karris thought it would be funny to put a spell on a Sial. It saw him coming, and picked him up and ...

"They killed him."

"They didn't kill him!"

Axe sighed.

"They almost did."

"They just ..." Elisia couldn't say it. Her voice faded out.

"Made him lose his mind?"

Elisia looked at the Sials, they were coal black mist. But the mist had shaped them out, they were shadows, but not stuck to the floor. They had claws that were long and dark, fingers that were equally so, and no thumbs. Their arms were longer than they should be … no legs, just mists. They were half dead, half alive … living off the common sense and sanity of others.

In old texts, it explains how Sials were created. It is said that your shadow is your evil side, the side that literally, hides in the dark. Sials were the shadows of the insane and corrupt after they had died, but had been too evil to rest. They say, that Sials are forever cursed to walk among the living … until the end of time.

Elisia looked at the Sials, they were coal black mist. But the mist had shaped them out, they were shadows, but not stuck to the floor. They were half dead, half alive … living off the common sense and sanity of others.

Elisia flipped through the pages of her mums spell book, until she came to the word Sial. She read aloud: EXTREMELY DANGEROUS: AVOID AT ALL COSTS.

Elisia looked at the book in confusion, is it possible that the book could be mocking her?

"Well, that's a help!" Whispered Axe angrily.

"Axe! We can! Don't you see the gap between them?"

"No, I don't see. Now let's leave before –"

Suddenly the Sials looked around them, Elisa and Axe grabbed each other's arms fearful, they prayed that they weren't the ones that had set the Sials off. Thankfully, the Sials didn't look their way, or it seemed, they didn't.

Loosing go of her friend, Elisa smiled at her…and stepped forwards.

"Elisa! What are you doing!" Axe whispered at her furiously, "This is stupid!"

"Stupidity is the key to invincibility." Elisa whispered back, taking another cautious, shaky step.

Axe gasped, "Elisa! Stop it! You're going to get yourself killed!"

But she wouldn't.

Closer and closer, until she was in arms reach. If it suddenly turned round and grabbed her, she wouldn't be able to get out.

Trapped forever.

Thump went her heart, thump went her heart.

One more step and she was next to the Sial.

She stepped.

The Sial she was next to didn't move; it even looked a little transparent.

She stood still. Transparent? No, it couldn't be …

The Sial next to her turned its head towards her.

She froze, trembling where she stood.

Axe gasped.

But it made no action.

It didn't touch her, just glared.

In time, it resumed its position and Elisa strode forwards three more times, until she was out of reach.

She beckoned Axe over and waited for her friend to come as well.

"I've noticed something," Axe said, beaming to be still alive. "They seem to do the same motion all the time."

Invisible, they both ran towards the window of the office. It was empty.

"El! We're too late!"

Elisia couldn't believe it, after everything, they were too late. It didn't make sense, they were on time. The meeting should have started.

That's when someone dimly walked past the window.

"Duck!"

They crouched down quickly, and turned to each other.

"Axe, remember it's the Spies. There invisible, see! Look, that teacup just moved. And there!

That chair has a dent in the bottom of it, someone's sitting there."

Axe looked, and soon she nodded in agreement.

"Right, let's put the spells … By the way, where's your wand?"

In the fastest voice Elisia had ever done, she began to explain why she no longer had her wand.

"Ok, tell me more after. Where's your mum's book?"

Elisia brought out her mother's spell book, "right here!"

Axe tapped the wall and whispered, "diaphanum". The wall began to ripple at if it was water, then soon, they could see through it.

Elisia cracked her knuckles, which earned a moan of dislike from Axe, and placed her hands on the wall.

"Speak."

The wall rippled once more, and soon they could hear all the voices.

Laughter, the shuffling of cards, the music, and chatting, all sounds became clear. The witches were in there too! Luckily, they couldn't smell (smelling is what witches use to sense things), as they had towels over their faces, something obviously smelled awful. Elisia looked at the table, and realised what the smell was, one of the spies had brought a rotten carcass with them!

The Spies where different from Witches in many ways, because when the Witches would gag at rotten things, Spies would happily eat them. When Witches would smile at a joke or laugh at a funny face, Spies would remain silent, when Witches would run in terror of a vampire, or creature, the Spies would befriend it!

"Look!" Axe lightly tapped her on the arm, someone was entering.

"Hello Marcellus."

"Good evening."

"Greetings, Marcellus."

An old man scuffled his feet across the floor, he had a willow walking sick, grey hair that went down to his shoulders, and, apart from the square glasses that he was wearing, a bare face, Elisia kind of thought that a beard really belonged there. She was about to voice this opinion to Axe when the old man began to speak.

"Greetings, Witches and Spies, I have much news to share. So I require you listen closely. You shall eat, but after I have spoken."

"Sir? Will you be joining us?"

Marcellus looked over at the empty space, and smiled.

"I shall not, I have invaded the time of these witches enough already, and I shall not cause more havoc and exertion." He continued, "Anyway, I voyaged to the far land of Ocluvard, down across the river of Zak and through the mountain of darkness, until I found the *divina oraculi*."

Everyone in the room seemed to be listening; even the Witches (still holding the towels over their noses, thank goodness!) were listening hard.

"As I looked into the shadows," He whittled on, "my men were gone, they fled after one of them went missing … I heard a voice, an echo. I almost turned and fled, but I felt a hand grip upon my shoulder, and then I fell asleep."

Elisia managed to whisper quietly, "because that's heroic."

This earned a muffled giggle from Axe and a hush.

"When I awoke, I was back where I began, all my men where there, but the only difference was I had a locket around my neck."

"Now, you may not believe such a tale, but I shall leave you to think about it."

The room suddenly filled with chatter, and Elisia turned to Axe.

"Elisia, quick we got to move! Now!"

"Why?" Questioned Elisia.

"That Spy just sensed me!" She pointed at the one in the chair.

Elisa got to her feet as quick as she could, and running down the small slope, she stumbled. She fell down the slope, straight into an awaiting Sial.

Chapter Six

Run!

$\mathcal{C}$lisia fell to the floor with a massive thud, and curling herself in a ball, she knew her doom was upon her.

She didn't dare to look up, she closed her eyes.

"Elisia! Are you okay? Get up quick, they're just illusions!"

Elisia got up, she didn't need telling twice, and before Axe could say anything, Elisia grabbed her hand and ran. Axe had trouble keeping up and once or twice nearly tripped over, but Elisia didn't stop running until they we're at Axe's house. Wrenching the door open, she shoved Axe and herself though and slammed it behind her; she breathed and sunk to the floor in relief.

Instantly, she fell asleep.

Weird dreams of cloaked figures and giant trees trailed over again and again, until she was awoke by a tap on her shoulder.

"Girls! Get up! You'll never guess! Someone listened to a secret conference last night! And, why are you all muddy?"

Elisia opened her eyes and she saw, Madeline, Axe's mum standing in front of her.

"Oh, we went out last night, Billy Picket was playing up again."

Elisia looked at Axe; she nodded, as if to say 'good call'. Axe went on:

"We heard him we did, he was trying to... climb up the Lignum Tree and ..."

Elisia, realising Axe had lost her lying streak, stepped in.

"He was trying to chop it down, stupid brat, we got him though, we won't have any more trouble from him for a while."

Madeline smiled.

"Glad to hear it girls, you must of been so tired, no wonder you fell asleep by the door, that boy can be a handful! Come to the table, I'll tell you more about this. It's in the paper!"

Axe looked at Elisia in alarm, newspaper meant pictures, pictures of them, them in pictures, meant busted.

Elisia looked down at the newspaper, and too her amazement, they weren't of her and Axe.

They we're of ...

"I know, totally barbaric, that Harley Marlow, and his sister, had tried to listen to the meeting!"

"Yeah, totally." Axe whispered, clearly as amazed as Elisia they hadn't been caught.

"Them! Gosh, they seemed little angels!"

Elisia smiled.

"Oh they're not, they're little horrors!"

Axe smiled too.

"Yeah! Horrible! They insulted the clan queen, didn't they El?"

"Yes Axe, and they tripped up their mother!"

"They even beat up a little kid! Do you remember that Elisia?!"

"Yes, I do remember that! It was ABSOLUTELY vile."

"Absolutely!"

"Horrible!" They said together.

Madeline raised her eye brows in shock and picked up the paper to read further into the story.

And, with that, they walked out into the kitchen, and gave each other a wink.

*****

"What do you want for breakfast?"

"Lunch don't you mean?" Said Madeline, walking into the kitchen.

"WHAT?!" Elisia shouted.

"What's up?" Asked Axe.

"The Lesson!"

"Let me give you some …"

"No time!"

Elisia ran out the door just as she heard Axe say "Toast …" Elisia ran as fast as her feet would carry her, she knew perfectly well she looked like a stray dog. She didn't have any time to brush her hair into that French plait she always did. None of that mattered now, she just needed to get there as fast as she could. Then she froze solid, lost in a dangerous thought. Wouldn't a little magic do the trick? She had no parents, no one to tell her she couldn't until a certain time, and she had been good enough to have her wand discarded.

She put her hand inside the shoulder bag she kept her mother's book in, and took it out.

She stared at it; the cover still had a few rips in it, and was still as black as the night sky. Then she noticed something, where was the lock?

She looked in her bag, the floor, even inside the book; the lock was nowhere to be found. It doesn't matter … thought Elisia, it's just a lock.

And, forgetting what she had brought the book out for, put it away in the shoulder bag and ran like the wind.

She managed to get into the palace court room just in time, well, she was five minutes late, but it seemed that Poppy was late too.

"Hello? Is anyone here?" Elisia called, slipping into the room quietly. The echo rounded round the room and came back to hit her own ears.

No one answered, she put her bag down at the side of the room, it was just in fact a 'room', and nothing was in it, apart from the stage.

Elisia moved closer to the stage, but then she heard the door open.

She spun round, no one was there. She wasn't fooled, she shot a spell at the door hinges, and it came down and landed on whatever was in the room.

The door had someone under it, and that someone, was a spy.

"Who are you?" Elisia shouted, her voice chords vibrating in her throat. She blinked. Poppy now stood in front of her.

"Lets grab your bag first, they might steal it."

Elisia walked over and grabbed her bag, something tripped her up. She knew it was a hand; Elisia stepped on it and smiled as the person underneath the door let out a muffled whine. She then walked back to Poppy.

"Now, what spell might you use to tie someone up?"

Elisia understood, this was Poppy's plan, this was the lesson.

"Repolious".

Ropes dropped out of thin air, and then, slithered across the floor like snakes, and grabbed this someone from under the door and yanked them out from the crushing weight of the door.

"Ouch! Easy! I'm here to help ya!"

It was the spy that had helped her in court, the one with the accent!

"I'm so sorry! What must you think of me?" Elisia said, trying with all her might to undo the ropes.

Poppy glided forward, bent low, and let her slender fingers undo the ropes.

"Elisia, that was good, try again."

"What? I'm sorry; I'm not doing that again!" Elisia said, she made sure she added attitude. Just to prove her point that she really wasn't.

"If I may ma'am, I think she got the hang of it." Said the Spy, rubbing his dim red wrists.

Elisia smiled at him, but Poppy didn't.

"No, she must practice. Do it again."

Elisia realised that little Miss I-Created-Poppies was as cold hearted as stone, also added later that she thought Poppy was very arrogant.

Elisia left a little while later, the Spy, who she had to keep apologising too, wasn't happy about his rope burns.

"This is going to affect my magic!"

"Sorry! She kept making me!"

This was in fact true; Elisia was made to do it. And then, took a leap of faith while the Spy escorted her to Axe's house.

"Hear about the listening in? It's all over the paper! That must have been some expert eh!"

He froze.

"Yea', I suppose it was."

He carried on walking.

"What's wrong?"

Suddenly a hand slammed into her shoulder, she stumbled back into a wall.

"You never say another word about that alright? It was embarrassin' enough without snot nosed little witches stickin' their heads in. Damn them all."

Then he let her go, and walked away.

Elisia slid down the wall and sat there, for how long she wasn't sure.

But it seemed to her now, that she really couldn't judge a book by its cover; or a personality to a friendly face.

Chapter Seven

What A Surprise ...

$\mathcal{E}$lisia returned to Axe's house, only to tell them she was going home for a night or two, and here she was, walking home.

What had happened while she was away? Would anyone tell her anyway? If something had happened that is, for all she knew it could have been a normal year.

But, if it had, why was she now, walking home alone? If it was as usual her and Axe would be pretending to sleep when Axe's mum came in the room and told them to be quiet, and then came in again and told them to shut up.

That would have happened, but it hadn't.

Then it occurred to her, it was only six o'clock, where was everyone? Where were the late night shoppers that were addicted to buying things? Where were the trolls happily stomping over everyone? Where were the worried people, hurrying indoors? For the first time since she arrived, Elisia felt a deep twang of fear.

She hurried on, ran even, until she saw just why she needed to hide, like everyone else.

Trolls, no, they weren't friendly, they seemed angry. They were stomping, kicking things. Elisia stood where she was, she wasn't afraid of trolls, they were nice, sometimes.

"You girl, what are you doing here!" Bellowed one of the trolls.

"I'm going home." She said.

"Home? At this time? This is the time of the GIANTS!"

"Trolls." She corrected stubbornly, disguising her fear.

"Trolls? Oh, you must be the child who has been missing for a year".

"What's it to you?"

"Allow us to fill you in, young warrior. Since the time you have gone missing, us giants, we don't care anymore. We have to abide by your picky rules and not smash anything up, you witches are a handful!" Said the troll laughing loudly.

"But surely, that wastes your time because we can just fix it with magic."

The troll looked at her; he seemed to be surprised she wasn't scared of them.

"What is your name?"

"Elisia."

"Well Elisia, I shall leave you. But if we catch you out of hours again, we shall lock you away."

"Really in the mood to be messed with," Elisia said, "I'd like to see you try ..."

*****

Elisia ran for home, but if she saw a troll she would walk very slowly just to annoy them, which was actually very satisfying.

Eventually, her house was in sight, but she found her house had got one of those purple ropes around it. It meant 'crime scene, do not enter' but Elisia jumped over the rope and opened the door which lead into her house.

Elisa's home was covered in a thick layer of dust. She closed her front door, which (to her point of view anyway) was crooked compared the rest of the house. Wooden floorboards creaked under her feet as she made her way up the steep, circular stairs with speed and agility (after going up them all her life, she had no trouble running up them). Breathing heavily, she swept across the hallway and entered her mother and father's room.

One whole year of not being here hit her hard, she felt shaky all of a sudden, as she sat down on the double bed. It was as soft and unmade as ever. She hadn't had the courage to pull the covers straight for years, since it was how her mother and father left them before they went away.

An idea suddenly sprung up...

She looked around her mother and father's room for something.

As she walked in, she stopped, and looked around her.

One year of not being here, of not seeing her room or her mother's room ...

An idea sprung up.

She looked for something.

Now, that something was something she only just remembered. Something she saw her mother write in often as a child, something that might tell her where her parents went.

And that; was her mother's diary.

It was as long shot, Elisia knew that, but least it might tell her something about the trolls. The magic book was no use in this area.

Elisia searched under the bed, over it, and even in the pillow, but not a thing was to be found.

"It's got to be here somewhere!" Elisia whispered to herself.

And, as a last hope, she tried the cabinet beside her mother's bed, it doesn't open. But she tried it anyway.

Nope, it still didn't open.

Her temper was rising, she swore and threw things at the draw.

"Why!" She picked up a pillow and threw it at the draw, "Don't!" another, "You!" a pen, "Open!" She yelled, throwing a final kick at the drawer.

She smashed her toe into it and fell onto the floor covered by pillows, cursing again.

The drawer opened.

The drawer opened? It opened? All by itself?

No, it couldn't be. She had obviously imagined it; all the same she whipped herself around. But no one was there; it was indeed, just an empty room, containing her, and nothing else.

She looked at the cabinet, but alas! It had closed!

"Damn it!" Elisia whispered with frustration. What was the point of a cabinet, if it didn't even open!

"... Elisia ..."

Elisia felt a cold chill go up her back, the whisper sounded like a thousand souls at once. All saying her name, over and over.

She felt a cold hand upon her shoulder, and before it could say her name twice, she spun round and hit it straight in the face.

The thing landed on the floor.

A ghostly figure, no vampire of evil, no Sial...but nothing she had ever seen before.

Its eyes sparkled like the setting sun; its hair was soaked as if the rain had forever rained upon it, a shark tooth hung at its neck and its clothes were ragged and ripped. Elisia almost felt sorry for the thing. Almost.

"If you're coming to haunt me, I don't think that's very fair. I only opened a drawer!"

The thing just looked at her, stared, as if looking into her very soul.

"Not to be rude, but what are you?"

The thing let out a wail, and tears poured from its eyes. Elisia covered her ears as the distressing baby crying sound nearly ripped her heart into pieces. Elisia found herself awkwardly waiting for the thing to shut up; she wasn't sorry for it. She hadn't done anything wrong, she was completely innocent.

Silence lingered in the room again.

The thing traced letters in the air.

You're not supposed to see me.

"What happens if I do?" Elisia questioned, trying to keep the thing from wailing out again.

She was good at acting confident, even though she was dying inside.

I stay here forever, and ever ...

"Who are you?"

I'm the angel you can't ever see; I've been watching you Elisia. I've found you're judgemental, rude and take things for granted.

So an angel came to me, just to insult me? Elisia thought this over, still didn't sound good.
Elisia didn't say anything.

But you're not horrible, you're not like some. You realise the true beauty of things. So keep your mind open, so you can't miss a beat.

My time is running short ...

Listen! Listen to me!

Within a dark age,
A dark evil will rise!
Rid the world of that evil,
But never shall she listen to it,
Never shall she.

And then she vanished.
Elisia looked back at the drawer, it was open.
She took a deep breath and stared at the drawer. She didn't know what she was waiting for, maybe another angel or some sort of other creature she could accidently punch in the face and kill ...
"I didn't kill it," She said to herself, still doubtful.
Carefully, she took out her mother's diary.
It was thick, and heavy. Loose pages clung to those which were still stuck together; there was a thick leather black belt round it. One of her father's ...
Elisia didn't dare close the drawer, she needed it. She knew perfectly well there are a few thieves around here, and no doubt they have probably combed this room once already.

She looked back at where the angel had been; maybe it *was* her fault it died?

She then looked back at her mother's diary, no, she had more important things to worry about.

"I'm sure Selphina won't mind the loss of one of her own."

Sitting on the bed, she opened the diary slowly, she didn't want any of the pages falling out and losing their place.

The first page was a drawing, the second was pictures, and the third was a small paragraph. These we're the things she had written in when she was a child, thought Elisia. So she skipped to the back, and read:

Dear Diary,
What a day! Jason brought me a cup of tea this morning, as you can see I spilled it over the pages. Sorry about that. Elisia kicked off this morning and Jason calmed her down so easily that I would have got jealous!

Jason, her father … Elisia's heart thumped hard, she turned a thick layer of pages before reading again.

Dear Diary,
Things are getting manic, the trolls are going on strike now, and it's awful.
Jason isn't replying when I call him through spells,
He's been gone for days now.

So her father went missing first?

It's getting too worrying to handle, he said he was going to find a legend, the Legend of the Lost Locket. I've heard of it, but I didn't think it mattered.

So her mother didn't care for Legends' and Fairy tales either? Elisia turned a few more pages ...

Dear Diary,
Everyone's forgotten him, even Sara has.
And she always had a thing for him, I must search for him myself, I'll leave Elisia at Kerkavia's house, she'll look after her.

So, her mother went in search of her father, and never came back.

Chapter Eight

Missing

$\mathcal{E}$ lisia took the diary with frustration, and shook it hard. All the pages fell out and lost their place, but she didn't care. She had studied the book for days on end now, and there was nothing to point out which way her mother had gone.

She threw it across the room and it crashed against the wall, and then fell to the floor.

Elisia opened the drawer so angrily that the whole thing fell out and turned over.

"What's the point of a diary if it hasn't even got any information in it?"

She was angry. Would it kill people to sign names when they write their diaries, really, would it?

"**Elisia**! Come out here please!"

Kerkavia had been asking her for days too, she'd stubbornly refused due to the fact Kerkavia was just going to drag her off to those pathetic magic lessons.

Elisia ran towards a window and opened it, then stuck her head out and shouted "With all due respect Kerkavia, I aren't going to them magic lessons. The next time you ask, I will not say it politely."

Then with a huge bang, slammed the window shut and sat on the floor with her fingers in her ears.

"Like a stupid child."

Elisia withdrew her fingers and listened again.

However, the voice didn't repeat and she didn't hear what it had said.

Deciding that now was the time to get out the house, she ran with all her might to the door and grasped the handle, pausing for a moment to listen, and then hearing nothing but empty air, she relaxed, and went out the back door as silently as possible.

But she didn't feel right, it was as if she felt lost, unwanted, not needed here. She found herself wandering around the shops, looking at her reflection but not wanting it to be there. Everything had changed since she was here, everything was manic ...

"Well, I'd be bloody damned, it's Elisia. You alright kid?"

Elisia spun round to find Gemini, the Unusual Items shop owner, looking at her in concern. He was a handsome man, with bright, blue eyes and short, scruffy brown hair. He was wearing jeans and a soft t-shirt, with a black apron over the top that was covered in saw dust. He'd spotted Elisia looking at herself in the reflection ...

"Yeah, I just feel a bit low, it seems like everything's changed since I was here. Even your shop has ..."

Gemini looked at her with pity all over his face, he then looked down at the floor, bent down and picked something up.

"I know what you mean, everything's changed, it's like walking through a snow storm without a coat sometimes ..." he responded absentmindedly.

Elisia lifted up one eyebrow to question his idea. He didn't seem to notice, he was concentrating on the object he'd just found.

"What is it?" Elisia questioned.

"Not even sure, maybe you can come in the shop and help me look for the book which has this in it?"

Elisia smiled. Although Gemini was twelve years older than Elisia, he seemed to know how to cheer her up straight away. He knew she couldn't put down a challenge.

"You're on!"

She ran into the shop and opened every single book there and went through every page, but she couldn't find anything on this wooden shaped heart with holes in it. Gemini told her to go down into the cellar and find more books to bring up, but he warned her to be careful. If a book won't open or has a belt round it or has a lock on it, don't open it. It's like that for a reason.

Silence; it occurred to Elisia then how silent it was ... But was it the right kind of silence? She suddenly held herself still, listening intently.

"C'mon Elisia," She whispered to herself, "It's a cellar, of course it's silent."

She began moving books and shuffling through pages again. The noise rebounded to her hears like a dull drum ... but this time it was different, this time, she felt like she was being watched.

The back of her neck felt like it was tingling, it felt like someone was boring into her soul with their evil little eyes...

She shivered, and began banging and moving books again.

A whistle echoed through the air.

Elisia whipped around, just to catch sight of a white blur moving past her vision.

"Trick of the light," She gulped, "J – just a trick of the light..."

She turned around, and went to grab a book; she froze.
A face was looking at her through the shelves, pure white and disgusted by her presence. It hated her.

"Murderer!" The thing yelled at Elisia, "**Murderer, murderer, murderer!**" It sang, right in her face, coming ever closer:

"G - ge ... n ... s ... **Gem!**" She yelled finally finding her voice,

"**Gem!**"

"**Murderer, murderer, murderer!**"

It suddenly screamed loudly and headed for her, but Elisia's scream seemed to outdo its scream. She screamed so loud she was sure people in other universes would have heard it. She wrenched herself up the stairs, and opened the door and through herself through it.

"Find anything?"

Elisia showed the chain to Gemini and told him about the ghost.

He laughed at her, "Ghosts? Don't be stupid! 'Course not!"

"But there was! There really was! A face, staring at me. It went too grab me for crumbs sake!"

"Did the scary ghost tie that chain round you then? Eh?"

"No but …"

"Did the scary ghost turn off the lights in there?"

"No, that was me I wanted to…"

"Did the scary ghost …"

"**No**, it bloody well **didn't**!"

"Elisia calm down! It seems really unlikely! That's all I'm saying kiddo!"

"Before you would have believed me! Before you would have gone down into the cellar and helped me look for it! But now you're not! You've changed. You're nothing but a coward!"

The words tumbled out her mouth before she could stop them, and when she had done, she breathed out and regretted every word.

Gemini slammed the book shut and looked down at the floor with a painful expression on his face.

"No, I am not Elisia. I'm just keeping you and myself damn safe."

Elisia scowled at him as he looked her straight in the eye.

"You went missing for a year, how did you think I'd react?" He said, running his hands through his hair.

Elisia's scowl faded, as well as any leftover anger. Her guilt hit high levels as she saw how upset she'd made him.

"Why has everyone else changed except me?" She wined.

Gemini smiled.

"Doesn't make sense does it?" He said. "It's getting late, I'll walk you back, don't want them trolls getting you!"

Elisia slowly shook her head in disagreement. "No, I'll go home by myself."

Elisia walked out the shop, rounded the corner then ran for her life. Scared to death of what was happening to her world.

*****

The next morning Gemini rounded the corner too look for Elisia. He tried her home, Axe's, Lignum tree … everything. Where the hell was she?

He looked round.

As he was walking round the town square, he saw his shop and stopped dead. What if Elisia had really seen a ghost? What if he was wrong? There no harm in checking … is there? Gemini picked up the pace and ran right into his shop, opened the door to the cellar and jumped half of the stairs. And much to his surprise, Elisia was there, looking for the ghost.

"Ghostly ghostly!" She sung, "Where are yooooou?" Elisia whispered, it was meant to calm her nerves a bit, make it all a joke.

But it didn't seem to work.

The silence tumbled over the cellar floor once again, the kind of silence that makes your heart thump and mind race with thoughts of death and decay. Insanity seemed to tick like a bomb as Elisia took each step …

"Rauh!"

She screamed and whipped around, but erupted in relief when she realised it was Gemini.

"Here," she gave him an extra light she'd made. "I knew you'd show up!"

"Elisia," he began, "Be careful, she's my mother and she's pretty bloody …"

Rapidly, everything went dark. They couldn't see. Gemini fumbled for his wand, and lit it up. Elisia had her hands ready, just for the moment when …

That's when they saw her, the ghost. She went towards them, with speed and acceleration of literally, an angry mother. She screamed and reached out for Gemini, as if she wanted him, needed him for something. Elisia ran forward;

fearless. Grabbed a bottle of the shelf she had ready, and aimed it at the ghost.

"Temilatison!" she yelled. The ghost got sucked into the bottle with a loud shriek, all was silent at last.

Gemini stared at Elisia, open mouthed as the lighting in the room began to get brighter.

"What?" She said, shrugging her shoulders. "I knew it wanted you, it's why it didn't get me yesterday. Good thing I got it, would have enslaved your brain to try and become human again ... evil little rodent this one."

The mist in the bottle seemed too react at this.

Elisia assorted Gemini upstairs while holding the bottle; he sat down in the chair. Elisia noticed he was shaking.

"Gemini, I'm going to take this to the Ghost caption unit, you need to come. I can't drive a broom stick yet."

Gemini nodded and took his broom stick out the cupboard; he flew Elisia there and back. He was still shaking when they got back, even though it was just like a bottle bank except the categories were 'evil', 'good' and 'mixed'. They only slotted it inside and went. There wasn't really much to it.

Elisia looked at him in confusion as he sat down in his comfy brown chair with gold studded buttons; he just stared into the fire.

"You okay?"

She walked over and sat in the exact replica.

"Yeah ... it just shocked me; you're a smart kid ..."

"Thanks ... just be careful next time. You were always like this in our adventures anyway, I did most of the work."

"Yeah, true that."

Elisia sat puzzled; she couldn't understand why he was so shocked two hours later. It wasn't uncommon to see ghosts in the witch world, everyone has the gift to see them. There was even a caption unit for them!

"Do you know who it was?"

Gemini gulped and looked Elisia straight in the eye.

"It was my mother ... she ... err ... died in our cellar," Gemini awkwardly smiled at Elisia.

"Nice, what happened?"

"Murdered, nasty business ... but she was a nasty cow ... she hurt everyone, that's the reason why my dad left her."

Elisia stayed silent and nodded at Gemini to go on. Sometimes, a long chat and a comfy chair can cure the works.

"I never grew up right; I didn't have the good quality of magic that you needed in order to become a spy. I knew she'd hate me for carrying this shop on and not following magic. But how could I? I was rubbish at magic. She's been walking around up here too, and she's been moving things. I think she took that wooden heart with her – it's gone!"

Elisia looked at the floor, she knew Gemini's story, oh, too well ... her own mother had been betrayed by his mother countless number of times.

"You know what? It's okay. It's fine! You're fine! Trust me, this will all blow over! C'mon! Let's go to a shop, go out! Do something!" Elisia exclaimed.

"Nah, not today ... sorry Elisia ... I might leave this place for a few days, go somewhere else for a bit."

"Oh! You can come stay at mine! We've always got a spare roo ..."

Gemini shook his head.

"I'm moving Elisia, to another world."

Another world ...

She gulped, "Which one ... ?"

"Contimipoe ... I think that's how you say it."

It was as if everyone was slowly backing out of her life, going missing from her sight.

*****

Rain poured down the windows, Elisia sat watching the rain drops, she couldn't sleep. Every time she closed her eyes she immediately opened them again, because if she fell asleep the time would pass quickly and soon she'd be helping Gemini move all his belongings too this other house. Not to mention the horrifically bad dreams she'd been having lately, last night in itself she'd had a pretty bad dream about a walking zombie killer on the loose, it even turned Axe into one of its own. She hadn't even seen Axe for the past few days, she couldn't anyway, she'd been too busy.

Elisia got down from the window sill and grabbed the roughest pillow from her bed, the window sill was getting uncomfortable, but she didn't want to get too comfy otherwise she'd fall asleep. She placed it in a suitable position and clambered back up.

She looked out of the window; one of the giants seemed to be heading towards her house. No, it wasn't a giant, it was floating...and it wasn't big enough for a giant. What an earth was it? As it came closer it became clearer what it was, an eagle. However, this was a magical eagle, not your usual everyday bird of prey type eagle. It was almost invisible in the heavy rain, but it's plain, dark black colour made its lightning blue eyes stand out. Elisia was not afraid, but something about its gaze made her feel like she should be.

She opened the window and it landed swiftly down on her bed.

"Do you mind? It's twelve o'clock at night and you're getting my bed wet, go shake off before you settle for the night."

The eagle shook itself dry, while still on Elisia's bed.

"You little brat!"

The eagle shook one more time and the young witch jumped on her bed wanting to grab it. But the eagle flew upwards and landed swiftly on the wardrobe, leaving the witch to 'face plant' her bed.

"You are as stubborn as ever, young Elizabeth, good, for I am too." The eagle spoke a low rough tone.

Elisia got up and wiped her face.

"Did you just come here to annoy me? You know I hate being called by my full name! What the heck are you doing here at this time of night, Gratis? You are a foolish, stupid bird!" She shouted as loud as she could, but it was no use, she could not hide her excitement to see him. Still, it was worth a shot.

"Yes, I am, and you are a foolish stupid child for thinking I cannot tell what you are feeling. I will answer your questions anyway, if I do not you may shout them in my ears, yet again.

I am here to give you some company, as your friend is leaving so soon."

Elisia felt a tear fall out of her eye, she wiped it away as quick as she could and sat back on the window sill.

Gratis landed on the window sill and stared outside.

"Tears will never accomplish anything, but you are still learning; you will know that over time ... a year has gone by, many things have changed; too many. Change is good, but too much change can be bad, you know that as well as I. After you went missing every world changed; Arroondera got the worst of the change. Everything is wrong."

Elisia nodded and watched the rain drops race down the window.

"You must travel to where Gemini is going, for he will guide you through the changes, as will I. I know this is a lot to take in Elisia, I know it's unfair that you never made the mess and now you have to clean it up, but Selphina has brought this wind of change ... and she has made a mistake. Every witch makes mistakes."

Elisia nodded and stared outside still.

"Child, sleep is most important."

She turned to him and tilted her head, a bit like a confused dog.

"But my bed's soaked, and my ..."

"Nightmares? As I have seen, they are very horrific lately. Fear not, I'll be here if you awaken, I am not needed for a few days, I will spend them with you."

Elisia yawned.

"But how will I know you won't just fly off?"

Gratis flew into the air and with a big flap of his wings sent a huge force of air towards the bed, it was dry immediately. He then picked up the covers with his claws and dropped them lightly on Elisia as she snuggled down, and as he landed by the window sill and closed one of the windows, he whispered "I am your mother's bird Elisia; I will not abandon you in time of need. I promised her I would look after you, and that is what I intend to do."

*****

63

Elisia slipped off to her dreams soundly as ever. Gratis knew that even though he was here, her nightmares would not fade. He knew the legends better than anyone, the legends of night terrors, and the truth behind their being. You see, Gratis was a magical eagle, he could fly in and out of dreams at will, and that's what he's been doing with Elisia lately. Although he could be far away from where she was, he could still open a portal and fly into them. He'd been watching the poor child lately, and he hadn't liked what he'd seen.

The eagle shut the other window and flew onto Elisia's bed, the thing would arrive soon, to bring Elisia another bad dream.

Gratis awaited for the night child's arrival with much patience, she comes when you least expect it. Pure evil runs through her veins, but she is not to be hated. She can't hurt you, in dreams you cannot be hurt. She has weak powers over Elisia because Elisia does not pay attention to her dreams, she does her best to forget them.

A floating black cloak entered the room, it seemed to spot Gratis. But it did not put the night child off; she placed two skeleton fingers on the child's forehead and within five minutes she was done. The dream was implanted; Elisia would awaken within the hour.

"It's a pity you magical Eagles do not dream, Gratis. I would have enjoyed tampering with your emotions."

Gratis looked at the dark cloak which was now stock still.

"Indeed, night child, indeed."

The night child tilted her head.

"Do not wake the child Gratis, or her dream will be worse.

I will make up more horrors to bend her spirit, possibly break it ... do not wake her."

"I will not."

The night child floated out of the room.

Gratis could not help feeling that Elisia was lucky she wasn't able to see the night child. Magical Eagles can see things others can't. They are taught over time about the night child, by the night child itself.

He cast his mind back to when he first saw it; he was just a little eagle then, in his cage trying to sleep. When a cloaked figure entered the room and went towards a sleeping witch, Elisia's mother, Mirum. Gratis had tried to fly out of his cage and attack the thing, he screamed and squawked. But Mirum didn't wake up; the cloaked figure implanted the dream and went towards Gratis.

"A magical eagle? Well I never. I guess you haven't seen me before have you? I am a night child, I bring nightmares. It's sad you don't dream, I would have loved to tamper with your emotions."

At this point the young Gratis had tried to bite the night child.

"No, no. Naughty."

The night child began to float away and as it did whispered:

"Do not wake her up Gratis; otherwise she will pay with a worse nightmare. Let the nightmare take its course, otherwise I'll be back."

It floated out of the room …

Gratis bought his mind back to the present time, Elisia was beginning to moan in her sleep. Gratis looked away, he just stared outside and hoped it would be over soon.

The moaning became more frequent over time, and then she began to kick, hit and claw the air and her covers. Towards the end of the dream, she was moaning much louder, kicking with more force, clawing the air more viciously and hitting her bed with all her strength.

With a scream, she awoke.

"Gratis? Are you there?"

"Yes, I am here."

"I had a terrible nightmare, why didn't you wake me?"

Gratis flew down and landed by her side.

"Believe me child, it's far better I don't wake you."

Elisia tilted her head, but didn't question any further. She lay down and tried to sleep, but closing her eyes was difficult, she preferred to keep them open.

"Do not let these nightmares get to you, they're meaningless." Gratis said, through the whole night he had to repeat it many times before Elisia finally nodded and fell back to sleep. Every now and again Gratis would fly up and send a big gust of wind towards Elisia, too keep her cool. On the fifth time of doing this, he remembered he needed a bit of sleep too. He had a long way to fly tomorrow.

With that, he settled himself on the top of her bed and placed his head under his wings. The night child hopefully won't visit twice.

Chapter Nine

The Lingering Mist

$\mathcal{E}$lisia awoke before Gratis did, she was pleased to see he hadn't flown off, after all, he could have. She got out of bed and opened her windows, another misty morning. Elisia thought for a while, until her stomach rumbled, then realised how hungry she was.

Breakfast was always served with Kerkavia in the Grand Hall, every witch was forced to attend, to people like Elisia (who were under the age of 150) they didn't have to attend … but, of course, they were always welcome.

Elisia set out in the mist to find out what the time was, she didn't care for watches. She spotted someone in the distance.

"Excuse me? Do you know what the time is?"

The witch mumbled something and walked off, but Elisia felt she needed someone around.

"Sorry I didn't catch that." She said, as loudly as she could.

The witch turned around and looked at her, "**Away with you child**!" and made a swift hand movement up. Elisia got thrown up into the air and backwards, she landed with a painful thump.

"I just wanted to know what the time was …" she mumbled, but she didn't pursue the witch.

.Elisia got up and went to look over the edge, to see what the Demon World's time set was.

She was just peering over when she felt someone seize her and pull her back.

"What an earth do you think you're doin'?" Came a voice from the air.

"Spy? Is that you? I thought you were cross at me?" She said.

She dimly saw the spy as he pulled her onto her feet.

"I was followin' you, what the heck are you doing peerin' over there again? What if it happens again? Deja vue?"

Elisia looked at him with confusion.

"It means to repeat, why haven't you learned French yet? You're meant too! See if you had you would of known that de ..." He faded out, Elisia could dimly see that he was giving her a apologetic look.

"Sorry ..." He said, "I didn't think".

Elisia smiled. "It's okay, magical beings often forget this stuff,"

The spy lowered his eyes and looked at the floor. "So it would seem ..."

He escorted Elisia to the Grand Hall, Elisia sat down at a table which was next to Axe. Elisia was just about to explain what had happened recently when Kerkavia stood up to give a speech.

"Witches, I have good news! The recent war between us and the giants has been resolved! How? Well! It took a big bowl of Limikist! As you all know, we all hate such disgusting potion, but they love it! It's handy for their cuts and bruises! So if we give them any spares left, they will keep the peace. Also we must all call them the giants, not trolls, as they get offended easily, and frankly I'm tired of having my rare potion making herbs stamped on!"

There was a cheer of agreement within the room. Kerkavia nodded and gave the hand signal to settle down.

"On to item number two then, ah, that's right, recently there's been a robbery from Mrs. Admand's store, we all shop there, if you see anyone acting suspiciously, take them to me immediately! Mrs. Carailie has told me to ask anyone about her snow leopard, its gone missing from its nice peaceful place in her garden for days and ..."

Elisia zoned out for a bit, these things didn't matter to her, and besides, Kerkavia always leave the worst news to last.

"And finally, news has come to my attention that there is a lot of tension between two clans, Timki and Annika have become quite hostile towards each other over the land of Contimipoe, which lies within the Timki boarder but spills onto the Annika boarder. We are told to avoid anyone travelling until such time where they are not hostile, please stay put for as long as you can. That is all."

For a split second there was a silence. Suddenly the witches erupted in chatter and Elisia began to eat.

"I never liked Timika to be honest with ya!" Announced Pietas, Axe's brother. Elisia had always admired his strong accent; he only visited every Arroondera every now again and she was never sick of how he spoke.

Elisia smiled, "When are you heading back?"

"Next week, but if the war begins soon I'm sticking around here for a while!" Elisia hoped he would, for Axe's sake.

The rest of the meal was spent talking about different foods and visits everyone's had; Elisia had much to say. She often found she had to swallow her food so fast it made her eyes water because she had something to say.

Eventually though, Elisia got up to leave, but Kerkavia was heading her way and frankly she didn't want to see her. Elisia panicked and stood just behind a group of witches so that she couldn't be seen, she edged round the circle as Kerkavia made her way out the huge doors.

What is she up too? Elisia thought, Kerkavia always stays for meals and further, why would she go today? Strange. Elisia decided this behaviour was out of the ordinary, and her best hopes of finding out the reason to act like this was to follow Kerkavia.

Elisia needed to turn into something which was fast over a short amount of time, something small but not tiny, something like, a lynx. Elisia looked all around her, the hallways she had come in while she was thinking was clear. She looked around just to double check, and then took out her mums spell book. Turning into animals was very advanced magic, heck, she didn't need a wand now, who was to say she was bad at it?

She found just was she was looking for at the very back page. See, she had to be careful; the first animal she is able to turn into is the one she is stuck with forever. You can change back to human obviously, but you can't change it once you're stuck with it. Obviously, the animal reflects your own qualities, and usually people only want to turn into the one that reflects themself. For Elisia, it was a lynx, she loves lynx's.

"Animalis: lynx."

Elisia felt a warm golden glow fall over her, she felt all of her bones change shape, a very painful process, but she supposed she'll get used to it. She felt clicks and snaps as her bones changed, and finally, it was complete.

The lynx sped off after Kerkavia, and hid under tables and chairs when people passed, she found Kerkavia's room, and snuck in. She hid under Kerkavia's bed and watched Kerkavia's feet paced back and forth, Elisia wondered why the clan witch was so stressed. Surely she should be calm? The war would not affect her, if there even is a war.

There was a light knock on the door and (what Elisia could tell from the shoes, and walking stick) an old man entered.

"Is it safe to talk here?" He said.

Elisia recognised his voice from the meeting she and Axe had overheard that time.

"Yes," Replied Kerkavia. "Where is it?"

She heard a muffled tinkle noise, and then it became clear. As if it was been taken out of a pocket.

"Here ... look after it Kerkavia. Don't lose it."

Kerkavia took a step back, as if she was insulted.

"As if I would!"

Then she walked out of the room and slammed the door.

The old man walked around for a bit, then said "Clever, Elisia."

Elisia froze dead under the bed.

"Come out please."

Elisia realised the game was up, she crawled out of the bed and looked at the old man. It was the same old man she'd saw when she listened into the spy meeting, but he didn't look cross.

"You are one smart cookie, I'll give you that." He smiled, "Complete rebel you are! You deserve to know the truth about the goings on lately." He walked towards the window and stared outside. The setting sun's glow covered his face in an orange light.

"Long ago, when magical beings first walked the earth, there was a man, a insane man, tortured from birth by a rebel kingdom." He shook his head in dislike, "He was not magical, he was not strong, but he was clever. He carved a locket out of anything he could find and tricked one of the magical beings into cursing the locket, so the locket trapped any scream of pain that the wearer had created. So if I was wearing the locket, and I killed you, your scream of pain would be trapped inside the locket for me to listen too, over and over again. You understand?"

Elisia nodded, he continued: "Although clever the man was, he didn't realise he'd created a beast, a beast which would eventually be so powerful that it would break free and kill him. On the tenth year of having the locket, the beast broke free and killed him. Another man found the locket and by the time ten years went by again, he was killed by two beasts, then the third man came along and was killed by three … you get the idea. But the fifth man who found the locket, had a non-magical daughter, and she saw the evil in it. When she was twenty, she stole it away from him, and hid it in a temple far from the world's eye. I set out to find it, but instead I found the spirit of her, and she gave it to me. It seems the beasts broke out and killed her, and she's been guarding the locket ever since …"

Elisia changed back into a witch.

"So … it doesn't affect women?" said Elisia.

"Magical women it does effect, but non magical women it doesn't effect." He said softly.

"How do you destroy it?" Elisia said.

Marcellus hobbled over towards the bed and sat upon it, and said, "Elisia, it cannot be destroyed; it is forever roaming this earth, one day it will get us all."

Elisia cast her mind back to the angel she saw in her mother's bedroom, she remembered what it wrote in the air. Elisia suddenly realised something, "Why did you give it to Kerkavia?"

Marcellus looked at her, then smiled and whispered, "I didn't. That was a fake, the real one is in one of my drawers at home, nobody can wear it."

"Can I see it?"

Marcellus suddenly twitched, his eyes went red for a second, his face smiling with satisfaction, like a mad man.

"**No!**" He laughed and laughed, loudly, mentally.

Elisia ran out the room and down the corridor and thumped her feet down many stairs, she knew Marcellus had been sucked into the locket, soon he would be dead. She realised that he'd had it for a lot longer than he had told her, and now it was taking effect.

She ran, and ran, ran all the way home and went upstairs. Gratis had gone out, hunting probably ... Elisia closed all the windows and hid under the covers, for once in her life, she felt unsafe, in the middle of the day. She remembered she was meant to help Gemini move house today, but she couldn't, she couldn't ... Elisia stayed there for as long as she could, until Gratis came back from having his lunch. She felt him land on her bed and slowly pace back and forth. That's when she sensed it, the secrecy, the distress, something had happened too Gratis.

The young witch immediately pulled the covers off and leaped out of bed, and put her hands in the right position to shoot a spell ... but her hands shook badly when she saw the state the magical eagle was in, she was speechless for a moment, but then she found her voice.

"What happened?"

The eagle said nothing.

"If you don't tell me Gratis, I will shoot you with a spell, and force you to tell me."

The eagle continued not to speak.

Elisia moved one of her hands back and forth, then side to side, then down once, she then whispered, *"verum de mendacibus"*.

Immediately the whole room went black, then white, and finally Elisia found herself looking out of Gratis's eyes. She was living his memory through him.

Gratis was flying over a land Elisia didn't know, he landed in a forest, a dark, damp forest which had the lingering smell of flowers and death. He waited on the ground, constantly looking around him, for what Elisia assumed was about ten minutes. A stranger stepped out from the shadows. He was tall, this stranger. His eyes were as dark as the shadow he stepped from, his face had one scar which started halfway down his forehead and ended on his cheek. His black hair was longer than usual boy would like, as it ended at his neck and curled up at the ends.

Elisia felt Gratis ruffle his feathers, he was in discomfort.

"Gratis … you still don't trust me? I look after Elisia well don't I?" The man gave a toothy smile, his teeth were surprisingly healthy, Elisia half expected them to be rotten, like a pirate.

"Tenebrae, you know I don't trust you."

Elisia felt Gratis inspect the world around him, he was in complete uneasiness now.

"You are still scared of this forest?"

A sudden wail of pain washed through the forest, making Gratis shiver with anxiety. The dark forest around him was slowly coming alive, the shadows were beginning to move, the world was beginning to awaken.

"Go." The eagle told the man, "Quickly! There is still ti-"

Another wail, closer.

"Go! " The eagle told the assassin in front of him, **"Go!"**

Tenebrae turned to him, sorrow flashed in his eyes for a split second. A word echoed on his lips that he would not speak, but he knew Gratis would understand.

Darkness began to reach ever closer, and the man stepped into the shadows. And waiting for no other order to leave, he cast the magic of his animals, and fled the scene as a fox.

Gratis was shaking, his heart was thumping hard. He seemed resistant to blink, but when he couldn't not blink, by the time he opened his eyes the world around him was meters closer.

Sials erupted from the darkness, silent, merciless, hateful …

They attacked, swift and cunning, making him bleed with their nails, their long, scratchy nails. He kicked and bled, scratched and clawed.

Elisia pulled herself out of the memory.

*****

She sat herself on her bed, trying to steady her shaking. Gratis tried to speak, but words seemed to fail him.

There was a sudden knock at the door, Elisia got up slowly, and travelled towards the downstairs door and opened it. There stood Gemini, with his bags.

"I thought you were going to help me? But you didn't! I waited up for an hour Elisia!"

She didn't say a word. Gemini looked her up and down, and she bowed her head as she felt a tear slide out of her eye.

Gemini carefully lifted her head up to look at him.

"You look tired, weary. Have you gotten any bloody sleep?"

Elisia shook her head, Gemini took out a bottle out of his small bag, he gave it to her.

"It's a potion, I travelled to the bloody Dark Wood to find it for you, it was hard, but apparently it keeps night chi … mares away … hopefully you'll sleep better, cheer up miss's! I'm never far away, I'll write as soon as I can! Smile!"

Then he grabbed his bags, and with one last concerned look at Elisia, he headed off into the night.

Elisia stood in the door way for a while, watching the poor guy disappear into the distance, but at last she closed the door … but as the dim clunk of the lock told her the door was firmly shut, guilt overcame her. She breathed heavily, with only deep regret as her companion.

Soon, she hurried upstairs. She opened her door, expecting to see Gratis looking at her, but he was asleep by the windowsill.

Elisia grabbed her shoulder bag and took out her mother's spell book, she turned the page to 'healing'. And found one to heal a bird's wing (any cut or broken bone on a birds wing could be healed with it), her mother had wrote it down, clearly Gratis had hurt himself before.

Elisia placed her hand out in front of her, and whispered in a quiet voice, *"aquilae vulre sari agics."*

The eagle awoke with a start and stared at his wound as it healed up all by itself, it made a few clicks as bones resealed themselves, and then the feathers grew back.

He stared around the room and found Elisia putting her mum's spell book back in her bag. Of course, the witch healed it for him. Clever witch, clever girl. He felt bad not telling her everything, but how could he? If she knew to much she would never go into the battle, the battle … his head ached when he thought about the battle that would end it all. He flew over to Elisia and rested his head on her lap, she stroked his head. He hardly let her stroke him, even though it calmed him and he didn't mind it, he had to make sure the girl didn't get to attached to him, it would hurt her more when he left her again. She settled into bed and he pecked her affectionately on the nose. Then he flew to the window. He didn't notice her drink the potion; he was too lost in his thoughts. But he did, eventually notice something was wrong when the night child didn't come, and when he turned around and inspected Elisia, he noticed the bottle on her table … clever? No, stupid. Her dreams would get worse the longer she avoided them; he took the bottle and threw it out the back window into the river. Stupid Gemini, the fool was an idiot. He did not know anything; Elisia shouldn't look up to him …

Gratis fell asleep snuggled on the windowsill.

Chapter Ten

The Known Stranger

$\mathcal{E}$lisia awoke with a start. She was panicked, scared. Why had she awoken?

Peering round the room madly, she heard a light scratching sound from somewhere outside.

The young witch slipped out of bed and grimaced as her bare feet touched the cold floorboards, it awoke her sensed further. She travelled over to the window, it was still dark outside, but light was beginning to make the dark fade away somewhere in the distance. She peered at the door and saw a fox, the same fox that belonged to the stranger, scratching at her front door.

Elisia woke up Gratis by flicking him on the head twice, to her amusement, he was cross. Eventually she explained that a man was outside, the look he had given her was worrying … but when he peered round, and saw who it was, he'd opened the window and flew out in such a hurry that he hit his head on the window pane (clearly ignoring Elisia's warning of 'mind your head'). He swooped down and greeted the stranger; the young witch stuck her head out the window to hear what they were talking about. Her dark hair tumbled out the window and flowed delicately in the breeze, it distracted her for a moment.

As Elisia watched them in silence, she realised that this must be Tenebrae, the weird scarface who knew so much about her.

Three taps on the door.

Elisia sighed, retired from the window and went slowly down the stairs being careful to slam her door shut. She didn't want to see this Tenebrae; he was probably an arrogant pig.

She opened the door and gestured him through to the kitchen. Gratis seemed to be upstairs doing something.

"This is the famous Elisia then?" Tenebrae gazed at her, unwavering, Elisia returned the gaze, equally as unwavering. "You're even more stubborn in person!" He laughed, his face was full of happiness and love for a moment. But then it was back to its normal gloomy self.

Elisia continued not to speak a word, she just looked at him. Tenebrae broke the gaze.

"Its useless to go on staring at each other like this ... let me introduce myself, Elisia! I'm ..."

"Tenebrae, someone who knows more about me then a stranger should really know," Elisia interrupted him in mid-sentence, "I don't know who you are, but you know me. It's not right."

The scarred face peered at her behind the head of hair, he gazed at her yet again.

"Surely, you know the stories of how your parents left you?" He whispered.

Elisia stood tall.

"This isn't some stupid fairy tale."

He sat himself down slowly, "You don't believe the tales? The legends?"

"No," she said, still standing. "I do not."

Tenebrae sat in silence for a minute, looking at her in disbelief. "You're a child, you're meant to believe those stories."

She tapped her fingers on the chair, "Am I?"

"Are they not a comfort? As you're an orphan?"

Elisia breathed fast, her heart thumped, her brain saw pure white hot anger.

"My situation is none of your concern." She growled.

He smiled, "Your parents probably loved you very much."

"Are you trying to irritate me?"

Silence shook the room.

He stared at her, his mind whirling, his eyes still.

"You should believe the tales."

"You should learn to shut up."

He raised his eye brow and ignored her comment, "I get that fairy tales are lies, but I am here to tell you the truth."

"You won't. Gratis tells me everything, I know everything I should know."

He laughed, oh, what a laugh it was! Elisia felt her temper rising. "Him!" He said, I am going to tell you! I'm going to tell you all the things your little precious birdy left out!"

"Gratis tells me all the things he can! Don't you dare say he doesn't tell me things!"

Tenebrae laughed even more.

"You actually think he told you things? Why hasn't he ever mentioned me? Why hasn't he told you about the night child? I'll tell you why! He thinks it's his mission to shield your eyes from the truth! He's a stupid bird! He's cowardly! Your mother probably knew that!"

Elisia snapped. A flash of white hot anger appeared in front of her eyes, it was all she could see, all she could feel. She forgot she was only small, and he was big, she forgot everything that she had ever lived by. She forgot he was a trained assassin. She launched herself at him, pushed him over. But when she went to kick him he grabbed her leg, and pulled her onto to the floor, then he grabbed her collar and pushed her up high enough so her feet dangled, high from the safety of the wood floor.

Elisia was trapped, what was she to do?

Elisia stared at the man before her. A cold, shaking fear gripped her bones and removed all anger she had for him; she now feared him. Fear entwined itself into her skin and she began shaking, her breathing was no longer steady, her heart was beating much faster than it should. She was frightened. She still tried to look strong, despite being hung up in the air.

He met her gaze. He was scowling at her, anger beat his ribs and made his fists clench; a white, hot anger.

She gulped.

His mind whirled.

It hit him then – she's just a frightened child.

He stopped thinking.

Slowly, Tenebrae's grasp softened on her, until she was dropped onto the floor.

He swiftly left the room.

*****

"Gratis?"

She opened the door and went through, the room was empty. Had Gratis gone? No, he was there, but he didn't seem himself. He looked upset, and as Elisia entered the room he made no effort to notice her.

"What's wrong?" Elisia said, putting a foot out in front of her then thinking better of it, space will probably make him feel more comfortable.

"I have to leave, tomorrow."

Elisia felt a sudden sense of shame, Tenebrae had been right, Gratis doesn't tell her everything. She walked over to her bed and made it.

"Tomorrow?" She said, plumping up the pillows, "Yes, that should be fine. I'll sort your leg out now then ..." She cast her eyes over the bottle, but it wasn't there! She went down on her knees and checked under her bed, under the draw, in the draw even behind the back of the draw, but it wasn't there.

She looked at Gratis, "Gratis, have you seen the bottle on my desk?"

Gratis looked back at her, "Yes, I have" his eyes lingered towards the place where it had, then the window.

Elisia caught on. **"You threw it out the window. Gratis, I needed that."** She ran towards the window and looked outside, as if she was hoping it had landed on a pillow and was perfectly fine, but it wasn't. She could see the glass at the bottom of the river, stupid Gratis ...

Elisia glared at him, he flew off out of the window, and Elisia got changed. She had decided that if Gratis was to leave tomorrow, so would she. This time, she's going to find out where he goes, once and for all.

She packed her huge bag and hid it under her bed, she placed her shoulder bag on the door handle and closed the door. Elisia then took out her mums spell book, and looked for a following spell.

At last, she found it, a sense of direction. She cast it over Gratis as soon as he returned and went to sleep, he didn't awaken, but she knew Gratis could sometimes see the future in his dreams, so she hoped that this time he didn't.

She fell asleep slowly, taking time to reorganise her thoughts. A lot of details had sprung up on how dangerous it could be following Gratis, but she didn't care. She just decided that it was time to find out where he went, no matter what the cost.

*****

Gratis awoke a lot in the night, he felt as if something was wrong, like someone was watching him. He heard Elisia's voice in the night calling his name, screaming … what was going to happen? Would Elisia follow him? Would she be unsafe here? Perhaps Gratis should take her with him? No, that was a stupid idea, he couldn't.

The night child did visit tonight, but it didn't stop and chat, it left. Quick as the wind it came and went.

He fell asleep again, but this time he had a vision. It was clear, clear as day, clear as light in dark. He was with Selphina, and she was silent, and then she spoke.

"Elisia … Elisia has set a spell on you Gratis, she intends to follow you."

Gratis fell silent for a moment, but a question lingered in his mind, and before he could think, he spoke.

"How do I remove it?"

Selphina laughed, it was a cold laugh, a horrible mean laugh, Gratis shivered.

"Don't remove it Gratis, let it be! She must find out where you go!"

Gratis looked at her, wide eyed, hoping he hadn't heard that.

"Selphina, she'll know ..."

Selphina seemed to understand Gratis's concern.

"I know, but its time she knew the truth. However painful it may be for you."

The bird tilted his head.

"Me?"

Selphina took a bottle of potion from the shelf.

"Yes, you don't like the truth. Your cowardly Gratis, you used to be a hero, you used to save Mirum. But when Mirum died you became weak, weaker than a magical bird should be. Learn your place in life, you protect Elisia now, Mirum's gone. She's up here with me now, leave the memories alone and focus on Elisia!"

Gratis awoke from his dream, feeling ignored and untrusted.

*****

The next morning wasn't that bad for Elisia actually, a little cold perhaps but nothing a good thick jumper couldn't fix, she set off after Gratis at day break. It was easier then she'd originally thought, she knew exactly which way Gratis had gone like the back of her hand, even though at that time she didn't know where she actually was.

The forest she was in at the moment was actually quite nice, the moss on the logs which were scattered around the place, the trees which swooped down were nice little trees ... here though, the trees didn't try and grab you, yes, they moved at their own free will but they didn't try and grab passers-by. Elisia had never seen trees like this, she still kept far out of reach, just in case.

But as night fell, the forest was not as nice as it was in the morning. Elisia could sense all sorts of evil living in the darkness, things stepped out of the shadows a lot, but Elisia wasn't scared, she had her magic, and her sense of direction ... however, when the rain kicked in, and the wind howled, she couldn't see and banged into various trees, after smacking into the fifth tree, she stumbled back and decided it was best to make a camp for the night.

Elisia took a while finding a good spot, high up, away from the floor ... she found it after an hour of looking, and with her magic, she conjured up a perfect little floating tent which contained a very comfortable bed.

After clambering in, she fell asleep.

*****

Tenebrae woke up just in time to see that little witch leave, he managed to set a tracking spell on her before she left. Then he followed after her, in quick pursuit. Stupid witch, or clever witch? He couldn't decide, she was definitely something ... he was hiding in the bushes at the moment at the dead of night, looking at her floating tent hoping a baby dragon doesn't decide to set it alight. To be honest, she would be safer on the ground, or at least near the ground, so she could jump out.

Tenebrae heard a noise from behind him, he slowly turned around and saw the night child leaving the girl's tent. He smiled at the thing as it went past, and it growled at him. Night childs haunt those who they want as their own, obviously lots of people wanted this girl, and she didn't even know it. Yes, the night child wanted him too, but he'd trained himself to sleep less than others without waking up like he'd drunk to much rum the night before. The night child stopped, and the assassin stood up, concerned for the girl. It turned around and came towards him, and stopped just out of arms reach.

"I have a message, from Gratis", it said, it's voice was cold, like snow on bare skin.

"What is that?"

"That Elisia must see this and you must stop trying to stop her."

"Okay". He sat down, the night child cast him one more glance (well, he assumed it was) and withered away into the night.

He imminently stood up and cast a bit of magic, it's been a long time since he'd done something this powerful, and he

83

felt a bit rusty. He hadn't needed it for his last few jobs ... he placed his hands on the temple of his head and whispered *"Profer dacia bris atramenti ollam, incendere pulchrae veritatis. Cover quid occtum es in obscuro protoium veum movere."*

He felt a power leave his body, a strong covering power.

Knowing he now would be safe from Gratis's prying eyes, he fell asleep.

*****

Gratis felt a power take over him, then he saw something in his mind ... it was Tenebrae, he was leaving, going away from Elisia. The eagle felt relief fill his body, thank heavens, he was leaving.

Elisia awoke with a start the next morning, the floating tent settled on the ground and with a wave of her hand it was gone, and she was on her travels yet again. The forest was a nice place, but she now felt like it was a little too sweet, almost sickly. She followed Gratis's trail with more caution then she had done before hand, because now she knew for sure that she was in danger, she sure hoped someone was looking out for her.

She rounded the next corner and froze stiff, she'd never seen such a beast before, but she knew that it was deadly. It was pure white, and twice a humans size; it had dark black claws splattered with blood, and teeth sharp and chipped. No eyes, and no ears.

Elisia quickly assumed this beast relied on touch, so it didn't matter how loud she was, just how hard she thumped the floor. She started backing away slowly, making sure she didn't move anything in the forest, she turned and quickened her pace, and then far from the beast, she ran. She ran so fast she stumbled a few times, she cast looks behind her but she couldn't see anything, and on her last cast back, she bashed into something.

She fell on the floor and looked up.

A witch stood there, she was pure white, like the beast ... but, the woman at least had a little colour in her cheeks. Her hair was tied up, it was bright red. Elisia loved it.

The witch placed a finger to her lips as Elisia opened her mouth to speak, and made a hand signal pointing to the right, Elisia quietly scrambled up and went that way.

Tenebrae couldn't believe his eyes when he saw that beautiful red shining hair, she was here! After all this time ... she was still here, Oculis ... he smiled to himself, it had been so long ...

He moved closer as Oculis climbed a tree and summoned Elisia up, yes, she was still as swift and graceful as ever ... he cast his eyes towards her face and felt his heart jump a little ... he scolded himself, you're here for Elisia, **focus**!

But everything stopped as soon as he saw the beast, it was approaching the tree and Elisia just couldn't climb fast enough to get out of its reach, he had to do something.

He grabbed his newly sharpened branch and sneaked towards the beast, as silent as his shape ... then he threw it, he threw it as hard as he could and the beast stumbled back, Elisia was now far out of the beasts reach, Tenebrae, as he soon realised, was not.

The beast reached for him and Tenebrae felt his death nearing, he heard Elisia screaming somewhere high above his head, but he didn't flinch, didn't move, didn't speak ... the beast froze its hand position and seemed to doubt its instincts for a moment, Tenebrae seized his chance and climbed up the tree with force and strength. He swung onto the branch Elisia and Oculis were sitting on and smiled.

"Right, Elisia, climb up to that thick top branch and sleep up there until nightfall, we'll wake you up when that time comes and keep an eye out for any danger, okay?"

Elisia smiled, and climbed up to the top branch just as asked, then lay down and stare at the sky. She drifted off almost immediately.

"Oculis ..." he whispered, "I'm sorry."

She looked at him and closed her eyes for a moment, then opened them. Tenebrae had always loved her eyes, orange with thick black rims, just like her shape. She looked at him with a soft expression, but then it turned nasty.

"You had eight years to tell me, and you never did, how can I forgive you for that?"

"I was sworn to secrecy, I promised I wouldn't ..."

She looked at him, then closed her eyes again and lent her head on the tree trunk. They were so different; he was forceful and mysterious, while she was open and kind, when she wanted to be.

"But I'm not like how I used to be, I'll tell you the truth. I promise."

"Used to be ... used to be ..." She whispered, and then she sang, she sang a song he thought she wouldn't remember, the song they sung when they were children, carefree silly children ...

"The wind and the waves become one with the setting sun, the shadows will roll right through. But we're not afraid, we're not afraid ..." and then she faded out, she didn't want to sing anymore. Tenebrae knew that Oculis would have loved to sing the end, but she'd lost faith in him ... he snapped off a branch and started sharpening it, "Just as long as I'm with you." He finished.

She opened her eyes in surprise, "you remember?"

"How could I forget?" But he wasn't smiling, he removed his neck scarf and she saw the thing he'd kept from her, he'd lied to her about the truth, and its time she knew.

She was silent, staring at his neck. A thin scar was wrapped around his like a ring, it was easy to spot, not so easy to forget.

"I was never sworn to secrecy, never. They caught me as I was protecting your father and they slit his neck in front of me." He paused and kept sharpening the stick, "I never saw their faces, and I knew if I told you your father had died you'd slice my neck again and again, so I didn't."

He went to put his neck scarf back on but she carefully took it from him, placed it to the side and inched closer to have a better look at the scar.

"The wit ..." She coughed and cleared her throat, then began whispering "the witches could have healed that all up ... you didn't let them? Why?"

86

"You know why." He whispered back, not looking at her.

"You bare it to punish yourself for not protecting him better?"

"Yes."

There was a silence for a moment, and then she passed him his neck scarf back. "I think it's time you slept, you look awful." But nothing in her face hinted she was in any way concerned.

He put the scarf back where it belonged and hid his scar again, then settled down on the uncomfortable branch, it was evening, the beast would soon be asleep. He shut his eyes and let his ears listen to the wind.

Chapter Eleven

The Cover of Nightfall

$\mathcal{E}$lisia was shaken awake after only an hour of sleep, she got up and tried to remember why she was awake at this time … after looking down, she realised the beast had fallen asleep by the tree. Oculis climbed upwards and jumped towards another thick branch and landed swiftly, she then beckoned Elisia across.

Elisia, obviously, was good at climbing trees. Climbing, not jumping from one tree to another, she wasn't a monkey. So instead, she used a hover charm and got there swiftly, Tenebrae followed.

However, she fell off one of the trees and bashed her head, but she got straight up and didn't complain, even though her head was throbbing painfully.

After that, it was really a matter of climbing and stepping, most of the trees were close together and it didn't really require much effort to get to another. Elisia suddenly realised they were heading in the wrong direction, they needed to go right to follow Gratis.

"Stop!" She whispered, and reluctantly they both froze. "We're heading the wrong way, see I am following this bird and I need to keep on track!"

Oculis turned round and looked her dead in the eye, "Bird? Blackbirds aren't that interesting, we need to keep moving."

Elisia looked at Tenebrae to back her up, but he said nothing. Giving him the biggest scowl she ever had, she turned around and headed in a different direction.

Nobody came after, Elisia was on her own. She ducked and jumped high on the tree tops, but soon she felt the spell pulling her, pulling her towards Gratis. Gratis? She couldn't have found him already, could she? But she had. He was there, right on the highest branch of the tallest tree in the area. She smiled, she loved high up places, and so did he, it was one of the many things they had in common.

"Gratis!" She cleared her throat, "Gratis! I'm here!"

She climbed the branches with ease, weaving in and out and using the strength she could utilise to get to the top. It took forever and a day (or what felt like that to her) to reach his level. She breathed, "Gratis I just … can I just explain that I …"

He didn't turn around or seem to register her, he seemed still … Like he was disappointed.

"Gratis … please?"

She reached out to touch him, but instead, he was knocked like a light object off the branch.

"Gratis!"

Elisia panicked as she could only watch him tumble down into the darkness. Why wasn't he flying?

"Why aren't you flying! **Do something!**"

He was swallowed by the darkness almost immediately. What had happened to the ground? Was it dark already? Where was Gratis?

She stared at the darkness, the abyss beneath her, praying that he would swoop up and tell her it was a joke … Elisia took a deep shaking breath … what was happening? She closed her eyes and began rocking herself, praying that it was all one big dream, praying that life really wasn't like this …

She awoke in Tenebrae's arms, it was dark, and she couldn't remember what had happened. He was carrying her, and after she felt her throbbing head, she realised she probably never got back up when she fell down. Tenebrae hadn't actually noticed she had awoken, so Elisia made the most of it; she made moaning noises when she thought all was a little too silent, moved her head a lot and tried to make out she was having a nightmare and once she smacked Tenebrae in the face when he was complaining about carrying her. Soon though, too soon, they reached their destination and she was put down in her floating tent after Oculis set it up. Elisia waited for half an hour before she left the tent again, she needed to be convincing, before she told him that she had actually been awake half of the way.

Elisia went out quietly, keeping her eyes low, and then sat down on the logs by the crackling fire. She spotted Oculis and Tenebrae sitting near each other, Oculis was treating a bruise Tenebrae had got from being hit by Elisia. This was her chance to show pure brilliance in acting.

"How did you get that?" She said, with an innocent look in her eye.

Tenebrae looked up, "You smacked me while you were knocked out".

She hid a smirk, "How … unfortunate …" Elisia went towards the fire and warmed her hands, her fingers tingled to the warmth.

Tenebrae patted the space next to him, "Sit down! I need to ask you something …"

Elisia reluctantly sat down; he leaned towards her and whispered in her ear when Oculis went to cook, "Nice punch, I got to say."

Surprised, Elisia looked at the floor and whispered back, "I'm sorry, I thought you'd laugh!"

That was not true.

He chuckled silently, "I did! I thought it was genius, I'll let you off, maybe." He winked at her and gave her a smile, she'd obviously earned his respect. After she had dinner, he sent her off to bed. She fell asleep happily, knowing that she was safe.

*****

The next morning held them in it's confused claws for a long time. The needed to leave as soon as possible due to the

91

fact the beast could be following them (that's what Tenebrae told Elisia, anyway) … But they couldn't leave without everyone, and that everyone included Oculis.

"She'll be back soon enough." Tenebrae told Elisia for the third time, "She won't have gone to far."

But even as he said it, he looked around the forest for any sight of the red haired witch.

Elisia … well, she wasn't as easily as convinced. So while Tenebrae wasn't looking, she headed off into the depths of the forest, taking twists and turns to heart as she knew he would soon be on her trail.

The forest did provide some comfort as she thought about the night before, how Tenebrae had chuckled and she had seen a glint of respect flicker in his eyes … there was a lot she didn't get about Tenebrae. But just as she saw Oculis sitting in a small clearing, she realised: She didn't have to understand Tenebrae, she wanted to.

Oculis was sitting on the floor in a lotus position. Elisia cringed, she could never do that. It was hard enough to stretch, let alone put your legs in an abnormal way and sit down … She'd never, ever be able to handle it.

A whisper echoed to her ears. Oculis was casting magic, and deep magic too. There seemed to be little she couldn't achieve with this spell, Elisia could sense it. It plunged into time and space, sending it's dark claws spreading all over the future, picking out pieces it wanted to know or show Oculis.

A dark swirl began to appear above Oculis, and with each breath Elisia took it seemed to grow stronger, and stronger. Within it, two figures could be made out entering a large clearing.

The smaller of the figures seemed to be hysterical; they were waving around and pointing at the forest like a crazy bull. They seemed to want the other person to leave, but the larger of the two figures would not go.

Elisia crept forward, determined to make out who it was … What kind of small figure had Oculis met recently? Who would follow someone else through a forest? Who would refuse someone else's offer to leave? What kind of idiot wouldn't run away from a crazy witch?

Elisia watched closely, each question searching for an answer within her logical brain.

She gasped, the answer finally caught in her grasp as she saw herself in the reflection of a puddle beneath her. The only child Oculis knew was Elisia, the only person stupid enough to not leave was Tenebrae.

So … what was going to happen?

Fear began creeping, seeping, feeling its way into her skin. She began backing away, feeling nothing but fear. The faster she backed away, the more the urge snuck over her to run, run far away from here.

Just as she gave in, she saw Tenebrae:

"**Elisia**! Where were you? I was looking!" He said.

But Elisia just backed away, scared for the people she could call almost family.

"Elisia?"

Then she ran, far away.

"**Elisia! Wait!**"

Elisia kept running, trees whipped her clothes as she ran, a branch caught her arm and cut it. She held it in pain, but she kept running. She was fast, and she was glad to see a clearing. Until she recognised the clearing.

Heavy footsteps behind her made her turn around in worry, Tenebrae appeared.

"Ah! Why did you run off?!"

"Go back …" She whispered at him, " **Go Back**!" She hoarsely shouted, feeling as though she could faint.

"Elisia … Elisia what is wrong child?! Don't be so foolish!"

"**Go back now!**"

It was too late, she was suddenly grabbed by sharp claws on her arm. They pierced her skin, she was bleeding. A tear ran down her cheek as she saw Gratis's glazed expression, "Your ill Gratis! Please … please …" she desperately whispered for a miracle, but none came. She looked down, just to see everything getting smaller very quickly.

A sudden jolt made Elisia look up in hope, an arrow had been shot, and as she looked down Oculis was holding a bow. It had missed Gratis by inches.

Don't hurt him, she pleaded to Oculis, please don't hurt him.

Oculis ran forwards and yelled words she never thought she'd have to, but after she saw the devastation on Tenebrae's face as Elisia was carried off, she couldn't ignore it any longer. She just hoped Elisia would forgive her.

Reaching upwards towards the sky, she yelled *"Mors circa angulos vulneravit omnem circa cor. Mergunt istam creaturam, cum atramentum nigrum art!"*

Each magical word commanded something Elisia had never set eyes on before, something so rare that not even the ground could behold what it was feeling.

Rising from the death below, beheld three inky angels of legend. A dark, inconceivable world crashed over their skins, bending them from time and space. Their eyes lightened like bright stars glistening far above you, but already gone out like a light. It was the darkness that beheld them in their wondrous beauty, the world around them which made them ever stronger, the hell within you they saw through. Fear feared them, life feared them … Elisia feared them.

They attacked Gratis. It only took one blow to make him drop Elisia.

Elisia was dropped, the ground was hurling towards young witch, what was she to do? She couldn't stop, she was doomed.

Elisia let out a roaring scream, it echoed through the trees and leaped towards the sky at a horrifying speed. She knew it was over; this was the end, the end of her life. For the last time, she looked towards the sky, and closed her eyes waiting for the pain.

But it never came.

*****

Tenebrae raced towards Elisia when she started falling, then he got himself into a position to catch her.

He held her tight as he watched Gratis plummet to the ground. Swirling and twirling uncontrollably ... the poor creature was dead. The dark angels caught the mystical bird and placed him carefully as they saw a tear fall out of Tenebrae's eye. He didn't know how long the ink black angels stayed for, but they seemed to smile at Elisia, but Tenebrae didn't let her see them ... or Gratis.

He closed his eyes and stroked Elisia's hair, poor child, she doesn't deserve to have this happen at such a young age. The loss of a friend, a family member, but they couldn't help Gratis now, he was evil. Something had happened, something had gone wrong, and it was all because of the ache within the eagle's heart.

Grief turns the heart cold, and Tenebrae knew that from his own heart and the effect it had taken on Oculis.

Elisia fell asleep when as soon as Tenebrae put her down on the ground, ache filled his own heart when he saw her tear stained face, but he didn't say anything to Oculis, didn't show it, even though he felt it ripping at him.

He went towards the crumpled body of Gratis and let the birds spirit free, and plucked a feather out of his wing, and placed in in Elisia's bag. Then left the body alone, in peace.

He returned back to the sleeping Elisia and Oculis, it wasn't easy, but he managed it, just about. He climbed a nearby tree and laid down, his thoughts swirled in his head like the ink magic Oculis always created. Oculis, the beautiful half ink angel, who can call on her ink sisters anywhere, anytime. He felt a stab of hate, which disappeared when he remembered Gratis would have never healed from the illness of grief. It had to die, it was fate, even if Gratis had to go with it.

Chapter Twelve

The Teardrops of Legend

O culis awoke after a dream of blood, knives and pens. The usual. Oculis got up with a lot of weight on her shoulders, her hair was down. She loved it, it was the only thing about herself which she found at least a little interesting, but even so, she pinned it up.

She walked to the nearby river, she was hot, the nightmares usually make her this way, but they didn't bother her at all. It was only the night child's playing tricks, and they were very cowardly. Dipping her hands in the water and putting it on her face was such a relief, they tingled on her skin cooling and soothing the hot areas.

"Oculis?" said a cool voice behind her.

She turned to find one of the ink angels floating behind her.

"Yes?" She said, turning again.

"The child, she's not safe here." It whispered softly, yet, the whisper echoed like a shout … strange.

"This is the river of the writers, of course she's safe."

"Let me show you, if you stay here for another day, this is what will come."

A huge black ink shadow (like the one before), appeared above the water, it twisted and turned until two shapes came into view. Elisia, Elisia and a stranger; who was it? A ghost of one of the writers who drowned in this river? It couldn't be, could it?

Whatever it was, it grabbed Elisia and went off with her on it's shoulders. The ink shadow disappeared and Oculis turned to the ink angel.

"What is it?" Oculis questioned.

The ink angel floated towards the water and seated herself down.

"Grief. It's pure white but it sucks the life out of everyone, you see it because we do, other people don't. Elisia's soul is in danger here, you must leave."

"How will I convince her to leave?" Oculis whispered, staring at the place the shadow had just been.

"You won't." It said, "Hurry back while she's still sleeping and take her away from here, when she awakens tell her that her mother would have wanted this."

"Why will that help?"

"Return to the camp and take out the book Elisia has in her bag, read the back page. It was written by her mother."

The ink shadow disappeared and Oculis made her way back, she awoke Tenebrae and told him to carry Elisia away from here, he did so willingly. Thank heavens he was safe from them, grief doesn't touch people who are closed up about their emotions as bad as someone who would show them easily.

*****

They reached a new camp after about two hours walking; Oculis's ink sisters told her when they were safe. Tenebrae placed Elisia down on a log and fell asleep near the young witch, Oculis smiled, he was getting more and more attached to the child. Least he was there, someone to give the child sympathy, Oculis certainly wouldn't.

Then she focused on the task at hand, carefully, she removed the book from the bag and flicked towards the back page.

A searing pain shot through her side.

Swearing, she dropped the book and fell to her knees, she clutched her side with a stern expression on her face. But she managed to look up to see Tenebrae picking up the book and placing it back.

"That," He said softly, "is not for your eyes."

Oculis raised her eyebrows in amazement, "How so?" She said breathing heavily.

He crouched down beside her and pulled up her top a little to see her wound, and then he healed it, without a single spell. "It is not for your eyes; it never shall be for your eyes and if you think for one moment I'm telling you what that book even is; you've got another thing coming."

Oculis got up with caution and backed away far out of Tenebrae's reach before saying "You're getting too attached to that child Tenebrae, we protect her, not love her like a family member would."

But Tenebrae did not lunge at her, he didn't even look hurt, he just whispered as he settled, so softly even Oculis struggled to hear. "Your ink black heart is overwhelming you; don't infect me with your coldness."

*****

Night fell over the nearby mountains, and Elisia awoke with a start. She forgot why she was here, what was the point? Why not return home? Elisia felt like she needed a little stroll, and she did. She staggered up and tried to clear her head, but soon she realised she probably wouldn't remember the way back to the camp as they'd moved around a bit, so she had to turn around again.

She sat down by a nearby tree and stayed there, it was very light when she finally got up and returned to the centre of camp.

No one was up, not even Oculis. Elisia lit a fire and stared into it, she wasn't even thinking. Tenebrae woke up after a while, and gave Elisia a weak smile, but she didn't return it. She didn't feel like smiling anymore. She didn't even feel like yelling or screaming, she didn't feel.

"Have you eaten?" He said, getting up and rubbing his eyes.

"No." She replied in a low voice.

"I'll go hunt for something ..." He said looking out into the forest. "Just stay put, yes?" Tenebrae looked at her one last time, and then walked off.

Elisia looked at the fire and decided to make something she'd always wanted, a cloak. Yes, witches could create clothes in fires, but only magical clothes.

"*Chlamys et umbra celare abscondere noc procure ex flammis.*" The smoke rose up in the air and twisted and turned, until a black cloak was produced, just Elisia's size. Elisia grabbed it and put it on, it looked good, she was proud of herself. It was nice and hot to, one of the plusses of making a cloak of fire.

Oculis awoke and saw Elisia trying on a cloak.

"Where did you get that?" She said throwing another stick in the fire.

"I made it." Elisia replied.

Oculis took some grapes of a nearby bush, "from the fire?" sniffed them, then chucked them away and wiped her hands. Elisia walked over and looked at the grapes, yeah, they were poisonous. "Yeah" She said, absentmindedly.

"Good ... wait? You made that yourself? That's skilled magic; did you do anything to it? Has it got any powers of its own?"

The young witch poked the fire with another stick, and then quickly dropped it into the fire as it caught alight. "It's always warm if that's what you mean."

"Ah, okay ..." The half angel sat down and started praying, well it looked like it, until she opened her hands and an ink swirl fell out.

Elisia came forward interested, and sat down beside her. "How do you do that?"

Oculis looked at the child and passed the ink swirl towards her. "It's a judge of character, if you touch it and it attacks you, you have bad intentions, if it doesn't, you have good intentions."

Elisia reluctantly stuck her hand towards it, it didn't attack her. "Can I learn how to do that?" She said wriggling her fingers.

"Only if the ink sisters touch you, but I wouldn't let them if I were you … don't worry! I can't turn you into one," Oculis said realising Elisia's sudden hand withdrawal and panic stricken face, "it has to be a full ink angel, but it's not your destiny so they steer clear of you." Oculis replied.

"What is my destiny?" The young witch asked.

Oculis got up and walked away, "I can't tell you that."

Elisia didn't question any further, instead she just sat down stroking her cloak.

*****

The meal Tenebrae 'got' for them was not to Elisia's taste, at all. Even after holding her nose it still tasted rank, so she threw it in the bushes while Tenebrae wasn't looking.

Pretending to chew, she asked Tenebrae what she should do, go home or stay with them? She had no bird to follow now …

"It's up to you Elisia," He replied, getting up and looking at Elisia's cloak (clearly Oculis had told him about it), "If you want to go back, you can. But I'll happily take you to where Gratis was heading."

Gratis … The name ripped her into pieces and clawed at old wounds each time it was mentioned … How long would she suffer for? How long would she …

A thought occurred to her, interrupting her damaged mind: "You knew where he was heading this whole time?" She whispered.

Tenebrae looked up, as if he suddenly realised his mistake. But no matter how many times he opened his mouth, no good explanation would come. Elisia knew this better than anyone.

"You're going to take me there, right now."

Tenebrae looked at her, "It takes three days to walk … you've already completed two of them in the right direction; we've only got one more day to go …"

"We'll be there by nightfall then." Elisia replied, stubbornly. She placed her cloak on and picked up her bag, still blissfully unaware that Oculis was after the information in it.

It was a long trek, Elisia's feet hurt by the time they finally saw the temple. It didn't really freak her out, she knew the story, and she had no intention to enter or anything … right?

She turned to Tenebrae, "Is this what the spies call the davina craculi?"

Tenebrae nodded, "yeah, but they always make up how they got here because it sounds like they're all big shots."

Elisia heard hatred in his voice, but she didn't question. Instead, she lay down and tried to sleep. After a while, she heard Oculis fall asleep, and then she heard Tenebrae slip off.

Elisia stared at the trees above her, she heard Tenebrae shifting around, he was having a nightmare … by the sounds of it, it was nasty, and causing him great pain. A question rose into the young girls mind, what if she was adding to the ache? What was the right thing to do? Leave to continue this quest alone, or stay and have assistance?

She sat up and looked at the dark path before her.

Leaving would make Tenebrae have less ache then she would give him, so many people die in her life, so many things happen…could she afford to bring him along? Oculis, well, if she died, Tenebrae would surely die inside too. He loved her, it was obvious. She turned her head, and stared at the floor. Her father went in search of the locket by himself, was it because he feared he would bring pain to Elisia and Mirum's hearts? Yes, it was … It was time, time she left. It was time she took her own problems with her somewhere else, and so it was, in the middle of the night Elisia left with her bag and cloak, hiding her tracks as she went. She did, of course, look back, but soon she was engulfed in the darkness.

*****

Tenebrae awoke the next morning to sweet silence – no bird song, no rustling trees, just solid dead silence. He pulled himself up and stared around. Elisia's tent doors flapped pathetically as a sudden light breeze swept through the camp.

Then a sudden thought hit him: "She's not there." As a flood of panic soared right through his body, he scrambled up and ripped the tent doors open –

Empty!

Gone!

He peered up and around, willing himself to think like Elisia. A cold breeze hit him lightly on the arms; he realised then …

"The temple … she's gone to the temple."

*****

Elisia slid down the last slope, and thumped down on solid rock. Bending her knees, and then straightening up again, she looked around her. No one was here.

"Strange." She whispered, studying the towering pyramid. Would her father be in there? Or hanging dead like the two skeletons on each side of the door rattling a warning of death to weary stragglers?

She took a cautious step forward, then another, and soon grew confident enough that she had nothing to fear.

It was silent, like the grave.

Someone was watching her.

Don't ask her how she knew, but she did, and just as she whipped around to search for the source, a spirit stood before her in awe. It wasn't unlikely to stumble upon spirits, but to have one not announce itself first was against magical law.

Elisia staggered back, in wonder and surprise.

"I bid you no harm," Elisia said, "I'm just looking for evidence of my parents."

The spirit was a woman, the woman from the temple? The little girl who stole the locket from her father so long ago?

"Are you the spirit of the temple?" Elisia whispered, not daring to take her eyes of the thing.

"You have one question, ask it quickly." It said.

Elisia stood up, what did it mean? Hopefully, she thought, it meant it knew everything. Although it was doubtful.

"Where are my father and mother?" She said, her voice shook with worry.

"I don't know that. Ask me a more appropriate question." The thing whispered.

Elisia was tempted to ask "when will you leave me alone?" but she didn't.

"Did my mother die or pass through here?" Elisia said, this time her voice was not shaking and she stood up tall. Oddly though, the thing wasn't looking at her, it was looking above her.

"Your mother died."

Elisia felt anger flood through her, such little information.

"Show me!" She yelled.

The figure was gone.

Elisia fell to her knees. Her mother was dead, dead as a doornail. She wasn't coming back, ever. She felt a tear slip out of her eye and wailed out in anger. This was all her stupid fault! She should have never left.

"This is your fault! Do you hear me? Do you hear me?" she shouted at the sky, as though her mother could hear her.

Oculis heard the yell, she had awoken the minute Tenebrae returned. They both split up and searched the temple outskirts, and now, she was staring at Elisia with pity in her eyes.

Her ink sisters appeared and tried to talk to Oculis, but Oculis didn't want to hear it.

"You knew. You disgusting creatures." She whispered at them.

All four of them shivered with anger. "If we told you, you would have ..."

Oculis cut her off, "told her? Of course I would have!" She went to smack one of them, but it moved and it was a useless air punch.

Elisia spotted them from far off, and froze. Suddenly she understood that they had known and not told anyone.

The anger consumed Oculis like lava running through her veins, she was angry, angry enough to kill.

"Oculis! Don't let this turn you; you know what happens when you let your emotions take control of you." They whispered, caressing her arms.

But Oculis was too angry to be near them, "Go. Before I spill your blood."

The Ink sisters left. Oculis buried her face in her hands. She didn't pay attention to Tenebrae asking what had happened. She fell gravely silent, surrendering to the guilt consuming her.

Chapter Thirteen

The Shadows of Yesterday

$\mathcal{E}$lisia wasn't herself, everyone could see it. Tenebrae, Oculis, probably even the deer they killed for a meal. But life wasn't the same anymore, for everyone. Oculis, because she wasn't on her own anymore. Tenebrae because he wasn't a numb coreless thing, over the days he'd suddenly acquired emotions, and Elisia? Well, she was the most silent thing in the world.

Tenebrae had managed to convince them to go into a bar in the forest, but she didn't even care where they went anymore.

Elisia didn't, she really didn't. Tenebrae saw it in her blank, lifeless eyes. His mind grew concerned, as they grew ever darker by the day.

When they entered the bar, the first thing that hit Tenebrae was the smell of ale and wine, the warmth and the knives glittering on the wall. It was natural for an assassin to realise that.

There was a boy in the pub too, about Elisia's age. She briefly looked up when she spotted him, but she quickly replaced back to her expression of nothingness. They sat at one of the wooden tables and Elisia buried her face in her hands, but she didn't care that people were staring, and neither did Tenebrae.

Tenebrae went up to the bar to order something to drink, as he told the barman his order, he couldn't help noticing the looks he kept getting from him.

"What are you looking at?" He said, just as the barman gave him another look.

"That child," He replied, "She ain't welcome here … I've heard stuff, rumours …"

Tenebrae took a deep breath, "They're just rumours." He told the man, "I advise you not to listen to gossips in the future."

He sat himself down at the bar and cast his eyes over to Oculis.

Oculis sat at the table worried for Elisia's mental health, she clasped Elisia's hand, and then walked up to the piano and sat down, brushing the dust of the keys and caressing them with love. She hadn't played for so long, but people said her voice healed souls and gave hope.

So she played a song she'd made up long ago. Tenebrae looked up when she started playing the keys, and when she sung, Elisia looked up in surprise.

It hurt her to sing words again, but to see the smile rise on Elisia's face gave her the strength to carry on.

Soon everyone sat captivated by her words and song, she filled the pub with her voice, it echoed through the small room and out the open windows, bursting to heal and help. Her voice carried everyone away, they felt the pain, the hurt, the desperation within it all. And by the time the last key was played, everyone's face contained tears.

Except Tenebrae.

She got down, her footsteps were the only thing to be heard in the whole pub, and sat on her stool.

The memory flashed before him, the first time they met. In those days, Oculis wore dresses more captivating then the Ink Sisters themselves, she always sung, and wore her hair down. She'd just stopped playing as he caught sight of her walking down the steps with people clapping her again, hair flowing, dress held in her hands so she could see the steps …

He never had the courage to talk to her that night. Never.

Oculis listened to the chat as it started to pick up again, but she never took her eyes of Elisia, who started to sit up straighter then in the past few days and (at least) give a weak smile towards Oculis.

"That was beautiful," Elisia commented.

Oculis smiled at the young witch, and was just about to answer when the boy they saw came up to them. His hair was (surprisingly) black, with blue, green and red streaks, it was short but growing long. He held a sword in his hand loosely.

"You're Elisia? I heard things, but I don't believe rumours." His voice was clearly from Oculavard, a nice soft voice, like a summer breeze.

"I don't tell strangers who I am." She replied, not looking at him, a bored expression glazing over her face.

He raised his eye brows, "Well, my name is Argentum, but most of my friends call me Argent. If you ever become my friend, call me that."

Oculis gave Elisia a look saying 'strange?' Elisia returned the look with 'I know?'

Argent gave Elisia a smile, then turned to Oculis.

"Your singing was brilliant, I've never heard a voice like it." He commented.

Oculis nodded in thanks, and got up. As she gave Elisia a look of ponder, she walked away towards the bar.

"So …" Elisia said awkwardly, "Why do you carry a sword?"

Argent sat himself down in Oculis's chair, blanking her question "Is it true you slayed the Night Slayer?"

"You mean the beast that's in the forest?" Elisia cast her mind back to its ugly face and horrible claws … but was brought back to now by Argent.

"Did you slay it with a hook and twist or magic?" He said impatiently.

"Hook and twist?" She replied tilting her head in confusion.

He stood up and held out his hand, Elisia took it and he pulled her up. "Stand still," He said, then he hooked his sword, "Like that, then you twist it like ..." Argent twisted his sword and in one swift move missed Elisia completely.

"It wasn't **that** good ..." She murmured, in a low voice.

"I didn't want to kill you." He said, then turned on his heel back to the table he had been on.

What a strange idiot.

Sighing, Elisia went to the bar and asked Tenebrae why he hadn't brought there drinks to them yet. But Tenebrae was in no mood to talk, for one, he had stabbed his dagger into to table, and another, he was almost yelling at Oculis.

"They wouldn't have recognised us if it wasn't for you and your wretched singing!" He yelled in her face.

"Excuse me if I wanted to cheer Elisia up!" She yelled back, staring him straight in the eye.

"Does she look happy?" He took a step towards Oculis but Elisia held him back. He was still fuming but did not push past her.

"Let's just leave." Elisia whispered.

The fresh air met her face as she swung open the door, and silenced the hushed tones she could hear behind her.

But something was wrong, something was incredibly wrong. For a circle of caped assassins in knight's armour stood before them, pointing each of their wands directly at Tenebrae and Oculis.

Now, you might have expected a little bit more of a fight from two trained assassins, but they raised their hands in surrender ...

Elisia, however, did not.

They began muttering to each other, getting confused why she wasn't raising her hands like the two assassins:

"Oi Kid!" One of them yelled, "Put your hands up or I'll clust you and your little friends."

Clusting was a form of arresting in Witch World, but it involved one of the most painful experiences you can ever have. Instead of arresting your physical body, it trapped your soul in a cage of deceit and lies. For as long as the spell lasted, you would live in an illusion.

It gave her an idea.

"Oculis," She muttered to her, "I need you to hum."

Not disagreeing at a time like this, Oculis began to hum, with each second she did so, the wind seemed to respond. It seemed to dance, ducking and diving through each and every sound she made.

"Do you remember how much Tenebrae just insulted you?" Elisia muttered to her, "Do you remember that?"

Oculis stared at Elisia, but the humming continued, and it started to grow, it started to contrast and develop into something more ... It started to swell into a weapon, just like Elisia wanted.

The assassins around them started to get nervous, and each time Elisia would remind Oculis how much someone had hurt her, the wind would begin to aim for them.

It wasn't enough by itself to scare them away.

"Selphina," Elisia whispered to her God, producing her sacred book behind her (the assassins were too busy focusing on Oculis to notice) "Help us. Scare them off."

Selphina began to respond immediately. The assassins started to get nervous, much more nervous, they started to be anxious, fearful. Selphina was causing fear to rip and damage their mind to the point where they started to back away, started to bash into each other, and very soon, too soon, left.

*****

Elisia awoke that night in a worried state, but eventually, she drifted off into dream world, vaguely hearing the whispering of Oculis and Tenebrae.

Oculis was not talking to Tenebrae. He kept trying to at least make things better but it just wasn't working. All he said was "Sorry, I was angry" or "C'mon! I was just panicking!"

She didn't want to hear it anymore, she got up and started walking off, but Tenebrae grabbed her shoulder and twisted her round.

"Listen to me, Oculis ..." He spoke softly, in a whisper. "Your voice lead me to you. And now you're here ... with me, I'm not losing you again. Not after last time."

She looked at him, how close he was to her, her heart was telling her so many things ... but her brain moved her feet back far away, it told her that he was going to break her heart, and her heart knew nothing. Oculis believed her brain, believed it with all her soul. Well, the remains of it. She nodded, and sat down on the leaf fallen covered floor, not speaking. Her heart had decided to make her tongue heavy, stupid thing.

He stayed standing and began to pace back and forth, he froze, listening. Then turned to her.

"When you started playing those notes, I remembered everything. You made me happy Oculis, you made me remember all the sadness, but you somehow make me smile about it. You make me laugh over my worst fears and I can never repay you for that. But I also remembered the day you went missing ..."

Oculis leaned forward a tiny bit, he'd never talked about this before.

"I looked everywhere for you, I went to every world, searching for your face, your red hair, your eyes ..."

Her heart looked up hopefully.

"You never showed up. So I forced myself to stop loving you, to turn my heart into stone."

Crash, her heart fell into the pit of her stomach and she was overcome with a feeling of dread.

"But when I saw you then ... saving Elisia, my heart beat again, for the very first time in 3 years ... my heart belongs to you Oculis, it always has." He finished, not taking his eyes of her.

She didn't know what to say.

"That's a nice story." She said, in a normal voice.

Then, she got up, and went into Elisia's tent. And with every step, her heart was screaming at her to turn around, but she never did.

Chapter Fourteen

Crash and Burn

$\mathcal{E}$ lisia awoke slowly, her vision was blurred as she came round. She moved her bones with caution, but no pain struck her, all the same she still sat up like an old witch with back problems.

She was aware of a huge amount of tension in the air, it made her weary of everything, any moving twigs, the wind, the rain, the voice outside …

The voice outside?

Elisia peered out of the tent, Argent, the boy they had met in the pub, was standing outside asking Tenebrae to see Elisia. Her.

Me? Why would he need to see me? She decided that the only way she was going to find out (to her dislike) was to go down and ask.

Sighing, she lowered herself down from the tent and walked over to them. "You needed to see me?" She inquired to Argent, completely ignoring Tenebrae.

"Yeah, I need to ask you something." He said, looking around with caution.

She raised her eyebrows but didn't question, she took his wrist and dragged Argent over to a couple of trees.

"This had better be important, I'm a little busy right now." She said in a low voice, crossing her arms hastily. She knew Tenebrae would do his best to hear what it was about, and Argent seemed to realise this.

"Ever since your appearance in the Whistling Redjay ..." He said in an equally low voice, "people have been following me around, asking me questions, I've only just managed to escape them."

He looked believable, like he was telling the truth, but was he?

"Show me." She ordered.

With a cautious look around, he placed his hand on Elisia's head. Suddenly, she felt dragged through time. It was a weird sensation, perhaps horrific but at least she wasn't sleeping.

Her feet landed on solid ground and again, she found herself looking at the world through someone else's eyes.

Argent ran, he was running from armed caped men behind him. They were armed with the latest wand technology. Argent kept running, Elisia could feel how scared he was, his heart was pumping faster with each step he took.

He froze stiff when he saw one in front of him, they grabbed him and punched him, he could hardly stand, and Elisia wondered how he was staying on his feet. But the man soon made sure he couldn't stand anymore, after another devastating blow to the head, Argent fell to the ground and groaned.

Elisia felt his foot being grabbed, he was being dragged off. He screamed and desperately clawed at the floor, trying to grab the roots of trees but they loosely came off ...

Elisia suddenly came back to herself, being dragged through time and space until she firmly came back to the present.

Horrified, she looked up and stared at him in the face, he had the expression of dread, and when she opened her mouth the expression got worse.

"You can stay with us." She whispered, it seemed her voice had failed her since she'd seen the memory.

A look of relief filled his face. Elisia and he walked back to the camp. Tenebrae looked up at Elisia and approached him.

"You tell me what happened, now." He told her.

Elisia felt like she had no argument against him, and plus, he had a look in his eyes which said "No arguing."

Reluctantly, she explained the situation to him, giving raw detail in the horrific areas. Tenebrae raised his eyebrows in surprise.

"Is it normal for them to go after him?" She questioned after she'd finished the tale.

"Naturally," he replied, starting to make his way back with Elisia trailing behind, "I suppose it's possible. Someone as young as him would be an easy target for information. But, we probably need to move from here, just in case."

She nodded, it made sense. And she was looking forward to having someone to talk to that was her own age and who understood at least a little of what she was going through.

It hurt her to think of the horror he must have gone through though, she closed her eyes and clenched her fists as her head became racked with guilt, it flooded her mind and soul until she couldn't remember anything else except her foolishness. How stupid could she be? Thinking she could turn up at a pub? Why didn't anyone warn her? Why didn't Gratis!

She clenched her fists even harder in anger.

Why am I such a stupid child?! She screamed in her mind, why!

"Elisia?" Tenebrae interrupted her thought process, "You alright kid?" he said.

Kid, yes of course, kid ...

Oculis looked up at her, concern filled the ink witches face. "Here," she said, handling Elisia a potion, "drink it, it'll make you feel better."

Elisia reluctantly put the bottle to her lips and drank it with two huge swigs, immediately, happiness flowed through her veins and body, filling her with a warm glowing feeling.

She smiled.

"Thanks, I feel a lot better now." She said to Oculis, to which Oculis replied with a smile. Argent smiled too, and then went back to sharpening his sword. Elisia sat down beside him and watched him. It was interesting, to her.

Midnight came with the end of the so brilliant potion, at this point, only Oculis and Elisia were up. The boys had decided to go to bed, its strange how girls seem to have more energy than boys sometimes. Elisia had commented on this once after the boys left to sleep, but that just followed with a heavy silence.

Oculis felt bad for the child, whatever was she to say to her?

"Maybe you should sing something?" Said a voice in Oculis's ear, Oculis wasn't surprised. Often her sisters gave her messages this way.

She began humming a old heroes tune she'd heard while sailing a few years ago, she couldn't remember the words, but apparently Elisia knew it because she began singing it half way through.

"We march, and march, and march until we beat the Black Knights ton, we'll beat them down one by one. Our swords are as sharp as our intelligent minds, our boots are as hard as our brave hearts. We march, and march ..." Elisia said in time to the humming. Oculis gave Elisia a raised eye brow look, to which Elisia replied with "My mother used to sing it to me ..."

As the days passed Oculis found herself wondering more and more what was in the book, and she was hoping that tonight, she'd be able to read the scribble left for Elisia by her father.

So with careful stepping after Elisia had fallen far into the dream world, she picked up the bag and looked for the book. But the bag was empty. Oculis swore under her breath, where the hell was it?

"Tenebrae has it," an ink sisters voice filled her ears, "put the bag back where it was.

Oculis quickly placed the bag back and hurried to her tent, thank heavens no one had seen her.

116

Chapter Fifteen

The Sword

Argent watched his sword with grief in his eyes. His father had died holding that sword in battle. He'd died at the hands of a witch. And that witch shall die with the blade of that sword. Hate rushed through Argent's veins, she will die for taking his dad away. She will, she will …

He was just about to pick the sword up when it started to rain heavily, and a face appeared in his tent. Elisia.

"Yes?" He inquired, but she didn't say a word, instead, she looked at him. Such fear in her eyes, such fear. "What is the matter?" he said softly, but she didn't say a word again, instead, she just pointed out the tent. Raising his eyebrows, Argent slowly crawled over and peered out.

A battlefield, a huge bloodthirsty battle field had emerged outside. 'I must be dreaming' he thought, even so, he turned around to reassure this imaginary Elisia that everything is fine. But she wasn't there. Instead, a women stood before him. A women with dark eyes and dark shadows under them. Singing a lullaby, and just as he went to open his mouth, she screamed in his face. And he fell, on to the battlefield, on to the memory.

"No," he whispered, as his father was struck down by a witch. "No!" and like the memory, he chased after the witch, taking her down and just about to rip the mask off her when … he awakes.

Tenebrae tossed and turned in his sleep, another nightmare. But why did it feel like it wasn't his? He was watching the nightmare, not being in it. He jolted awake after seeing the witches face. Why did Gratis show him it? What was the point of it? He didn't know, but all he did know was that Elisia was in his tent.

"What the hell are you doing in here?" He whispered.

"Sorry," she whispered back, "but I had an odd dream."

Tenebrae looked at her, could she have had the same dream? "What was it like?" He said.

"Well, it was a battlefield, and some man was struck down …" She whispered.

"Ah … anything else?" he whispered back. She shook her head. Tenebrae took one of his blankets off him and placed it over Elisia, "Here," he said, "Sleep over there, and wake me up if you have any more bad dreams". Elisia smiled and nodded, and went over and almost fell asleep instantly, while Tenebrae sat on his own, trying to figure out where he'd seen that face before.

Oculis sat with her ink sisters in her tent, they were telling her of a memory of Argents which, to Oculis's dislike, had to be incredibly detailed. By the sounds of it, the boy had been through a awful lot.

"So his dad was slain by a witch?" Oculis asked for the seventh time.

"Yes."

"And the witch was?" Oculis asked.

"Tympeli Callous; and you have to prevent him from meeting her."

The ink sisters disappeared.

*****

Elisia fell asleep almost immediately, and dreamed of Argents sword. It was so beautiful, but every time she reached for it, it seemed to fade and move away from her grasp.

Chapter Sixteen

Welcome

Gemini sat alone in his big new house; it was beautiful, and huge. It was difficult to not miss his old cramped one; least that one didn't feel so empty. Everything seemed too new here, the house didn't even look what his father would call 'lived in'… part of Gemini wanted to go back to his old home, but part of him wanted to stay here.

He slowly got on to his feet and walked around the room that he could imagine as his lounge. 'Imaginary', said an ugly thought inside him, 'pretend'. Gemini sped up his walking pace; he knew that running from his own self would never work, but that thought was to truthful, way too truthful. He ran into another room and closed the door behind him, leaning against the door, he sunk to the ground and looked up, just to hear the thought return and say, 'This could have been Elisia's room'.

It was true Gemini had long wanted to take care of Elisia, he knew she was too wild to be careful. She needed someone to guide her, someone like an older brother, and Gemini had so long tried to look after her, but she'd always just dragged him along too.

The memories flashed past Gemini's eyes, the river adventure, the forest, the light house, the ship, the graveyard cave … danger too many times, and now, well now he was running away. Who would take care of her now? She's probably all alone in that house full of memories, scared to death because of her nightmares …

He shook his head and got up, sipping his drink. Don't be silly he told himself, she's probably off on one of her wild adventures, getting herself into danger and laughing while scared out of her wits! All the same, he slammed down the tea on his table, most of it splashed out and burned his hand; wincing, he grabbed his black cloak and bag and went to Elisia's aid.

*****

Gemini hadn't expected to come in to find her in her home, but saying that, he hadn't expected to come in to see the thick dust settling on everything. Where was she? He'd asked around, and, by the sounds of things, Elisia hadn't been seen for weeks. Only a few people said they'd heard rumours of her appearance in the Whistling Redjay, but how could Gemini know that was true? It was tiring, very tiring. He'd asked so many people, he just wanted to sleep. He couldn't, not now. "Elisia's in danger!!" screamed his thoughts, "get up and go to her aid!"

But his body just wouldn't allow it, he slumped into a heap on the cold ground and let his eyes sleep.

He'd forgotten one major problem with this.

Trolls, or **Giants**.

*****

Tenebrae awoke with a heavy head. His thoughts whirled in his mind to fast to even try and tackle them one by one. Surely this was another case of the rejection he'd had so long ago. Stupid Tenebrae, you should have stayed a mean old person to Elisia, why did you show her your true side anyway? Why did you show Oculis it? Oh yes, because you wanted to be a nice little hero. Reality check, you're not.

Frowning, he managed to get up and out of the tent, treading careful of course, Elisia was still asleep. When he got outside, he saw Argent, staring into the fire intently. The boy was clearly lost in his thoughts.

Was it wise to disturb a thinking man? Probably not. So with each step, Tenebrae (again) treaded careful, until he was out of ears reach of Argent.

Honestly, he thought bending down under a branch heading to the nearby river; everything had been so perfect until he decided to show his emotions. If only he could shed this skin for a while. So, as if he was giving it a try, he transformed into his fox form, speeding through the trees with ease, until he finally met the river. Now, it wasn't wise to go drinking water, for one, Water Women could be lurking in its depths. They (sometimes) give good answers when all is lost, but they also (rarely) drag you in and drown you if you're not careful. So, how to test if it's good water? Easy, disturb the surface of the water; and with that, Tenebrae transformed back into himself, and chucked a stick into the depths.

Immediately, the water began reaching upwards, twisting and turning until a small see-through girl stood upon the surface.

"Tenebrae? You're lucky I don't drown you now. What are you doing this far out this time? You have far too many enemies." It said, pointing towards the trees.

"The shadows here don't scare me, you should know that Wateress." He stubbornly replied, not taking his eyes off her.

"Indeed, I do. I have a message for you, once I tell you, you can safely collect water." She whispered, "Wateress's honour" she made a bird with her hands and placed it on her heart. If she did not do as she said, that bird would peck her heart for all eternity. "The message: Don't go after Elisia."

Tenebrae turned his head in confusion, "What?" But the water woman was gone, and Tenebrae collected water safely, and ran away before they could grab him. Water women were sneaky, they would, stick to their word, but the moment the bird flew, they would be after you, trying to drown you.

By the time Tenebrae arrived back, Elisia was up.

"I got some water." He announced as he ducked under some branches. In response to this, Elisia nodded. She looked awfully tired. Tenebrae felt a little blossom of sympathy in his heart, but he smashed it up. No more would he feel for the child, silly child. He proved this by walking by her without a second glance.

"Does he always treat you like that Elisia?" He heard Argent say.

Tenebrae slowed down his pace a little to hear Elisia's answer.

"No. Sometimes he shows me kindness, and sometimes he tells me to grow up. He usually means good."

Usually? His heart decided to echo. Shut up said his brain, you respect her. That life is over, stop caring.

He carried on walking, until he realised he was entering dangerous ground. He was literally ten steps from being beside Oculis's tent. Would it be so wrong if he did? Yes, according to his feet it would be. He began walking past the tent. He always had to do the wrong thing, whatever the consequences.

*****

Gemini awoke with a sudden realisation that he wasn't laying on a hard cold floor.

No, now he was chained up high in a castle.

"You've got to be bloody kidding me," he thought. He was almost waiting for the witches to come out and laugh. But nobody did.

"Hello?" he dared to call out. Nobody answered him.
"So Gemini," he thought, "how are you going to get out of this pickle? Magic will help … but can you?"

He'll have to try.

"*Unocus!*" he said. Not to his surprise they didn't open. His mother had once told him that the bigger the lock, the more expression and emotion you had to put into the spell.

"*Unocus!*" He said again, this time with expression. Nothing happened.

"Emotion Gemini! You need to get out of here to **save** Elisia! She's in trouble! What if she dies because you can't do a stupid spell!" He yelled at himself in his mind until he felt the desperation building up in him.

"Unocus!" he yelled, and with that, the chains undid and he fell down to the floor below. "Hell yeah!" he yelled in his head, with a smile, he studied his surroundings and got up to his feet. There was a door over in the far side, but it looked risky.

Even so, risks are what you have to take in these situations. So he slid through it and hoped for the best.

*****

Oculis studied her water bowl intently. It was showing her three images and frankly she was really confused about them. First, it showed her a roman numeral (she thinks it was two), then it showed her a net, and finally, a little girl that falls through a trap door. She just didn't understand the first image at all, or what they all meant together. She needed Elisia.

"Elisia?" She said sticking her head out of the tent, "come here for a second, I need your help."

Elisia seemed to, reluctantly, get up and duck inside tent. She sat next to Oculis.

"Look at my water bowl and tell me what you see."

Elisia nodded and stared into it. "I see, a roman numeral. A net, and a little girl falling into a trap."

Oculis placed the bowl back in front of herself, "does any of that mean anything to you?"

Elisia sat for a moment, looking at the bowl. And suddenly, her eyes widened. "That's not a roman numeral, that's the symbol for Gemini, in horoscopes, something I learnt about in the Demon World … Gemini is my friend, he moved away." With each word Elisia seemed to get more and more panicked. "The net means he's been caught, but if you look closely the net has a hole in it. So he's going to get out. If you look at the little girl falling into the trap this way," she spun the bowl round in front of Oculis. "It now looks like a little girl reaching out for a hand to help her out of a trap."

It all suddenly clicked.

"Thank you Elisia."

The young witch turned and left the tent in silence, and as soon as she was far away, Oculis took a bottle which contained a bit of her own blood.

She placed one drop in the water bowl and asked "Who is this Gemini? And how can I find him?" The question seemed to swirl the blood around and around, carefully, she opened her mind and concentrated as best as she could. However, after hours of this, her attention just seemed to fizzle out. She needed a walk, refresh her soul.

Carefully, she looked around and went out of her tent. Light on her feet, she tiptoed past each tree in case it awoke and gave her a lecture on how sleep is important. And then she ran, she ran until she met the river. Her feet felt relieved when she put them in the water to calm herself.

Instantly a water woman appeared and went to grab her, Oculis froze her. Stupid things water women; they don't understand that some witches know how to beat them.

*****

Gemini thundered down the dark path, he took a sharp right as he realised the guards were following him. He needed an exit, a giant entrance door perhaps?

"Bingo!" He whispered, and full speed he pelted at them, they crashed open and he sped past the guards who were clearly keeping a watch out for intruders. They were so bewildered by the fact there was an escapee that they didn't realise they needed to follow him until he was out of sight.

Jumping over a fence, he pelted into the town square.

He swore to himself as he suddenly realised where he was, although relieved, it was also horrifying.

Ocluvard.

"Damn to hell," He breathed, "How the hell did I get here?"

Chapter Seventeen

Halfway Across

Ocluvard was the place of harsh punishment and strict rules. It was ruled by a gang, no, gang wasn't the word. Thugs, who managed to seize power with force, and take the land for their own.

Gemini think, he thought to himself, you have to get your butt out of sight. So, with care, Gemini hid in an old abandoned church. The doors creaked a bit, but it didn't matter, all the souls here had died from strict ways, they no longer heard the creaks.

He sat himself on one of the benches and buried his face in his hands.

"Think! Think! Dad would have said make a list of importance," he thought. He needed an order.

"One, get myself out of here. How?" He peered around the room, a cloak had been left on the floor, he could disguise himself in the night and flee. "Two, find a source of food and water. Three, find Elisia."

He got himself up and walked over to the cloak, picked it up and looked at it.

"Looks wearable." He whispered.

*****

Night had fallen over the camp, and Elisia was collecting wood from the ground. She knew she had strayed further from the camp then Tenebrae would have liked, but she didn't care. There wasn't much out here to harm her, well, she hadn't seen anything.

Frankly, she was just glad to be out of their grasp, they all pressured her too much, it was like she was a dog on a chain, she wasn't even allowed too far out. Had everyone forgotten her one year experience in the Demon World? Yes, it seemed they had. She wasn't stupid! She knew the dangers!

Elisia's thinking was interrupted by a growling sound behind her.

Stock still, heart thumping and her brain fuzzed, she had no idea what to do. Fear had made her immobile.

The growling had started working its way round to the front of Elisia. The poor girl couldn't even see what it was in the dark.

The moonlight seemed to shine brighter than usual, and as the thing pounced at the witch, she saw six legs. Dropping her sticks, she ran further into the forest. She couldn't out run something with six legs! What animals do she know of that have six legs? Catacomb's do! But they're just a myth, aren't they?!

Thumping sounds behind her gave her a sudden realisiation that indeed, the beast was following her. What happened if its friends came? Would she ever get out?
It began snapping at the witches ankles, and as the thing caught up, it bit her fair and square.

Elisia fell with a roaring scream as searing pain erupted up her leg. It pounced on top of her, she kicked and clawed, trying to go for its eyes. It was a poor defence, and soon, its sharp teeth sunk themselves into her arm. She screamed again, she managed to punch it in to face which at least dazed it for a second. That second was all Argent needed.

He came thundering down to the beast, and with a swift swing of his father's sword the thing wailed, and died.
Elisia really couldn't believe it.

"Now," He breathed, "We're even."

"Even?" She whispered, as the pain in her arm and ankle threatened to cause her to wail out.

"You've kept me from danger, and now I've just done the same for you." He explained, throwing his sword down he grabbed her hand and pulled her up so she leaned on him. "That ankle will infect if we don't get Oculis." He said, managing to bend down, grab his sword and use it as a walking stick.

"I can't go back there now, they'll never let me out of their sight again." Elisia moaned.

For a minute, Argent seemed to be thinking of somewhere else she could go. But he shook his head.

There is Ocluvard, its only about, half an hour from here?

If Elisia was honest, she didn't even care. She just wanted someone to stop the searing pain in her arm and ankle. But then a question rose to her head.

"Why did you follow me?" She breathed.

"Because I realised Tenebrae didn't." He replied, with a frown on his face.

*****

Oculis awoke to a searing pain in her ankle and arm, and all she could hear was Elisia's scream ringing in her ears. She hurried out of her tent and opened Tenebrae's, he had to know she was hurt.

But Tenebrae wasn't there.

He wasn't in any part of the camp when Oculis checked. She sensed for his path, and realised something quite strange.
He'd left the camp at his own free will, in the shape of a fox. She then tried to sense for him, but she couldn't feel him, all she could feel was cold.

Horror struck, she ran down the path he had gone, just to find a dead fox, with a catacomb bite in its neck at the end.

But something wasn't quite right, the fox didn't seem like Tenebrae's shape.

"Damnit!" She whispered, "It's an illusion!"

There was no way of telling which way he'd gone, all she knew was that he didn't want to be followed. Elisia, where was she? Luckily, she was still alive, by the sounds of it; Argent had saved her from the Catacomb.

Forgetting Tenebrae, she tidied up the camp and went in search for Elisia and Argent.

She eventually caught up with them, they didn't look happy to see her, but at least she was there protecting them. They managed to buckle down and get to Ocluvard in twenty minutes (Oculis carried Elisia which sped them up considerably, the poor girl was unable to walk or limp). They snuck into an old abandoned church that Oculis led them too. Oculis sped down a thin corridor, lead by her sisters to an equally thin door right at the other side of the hallway. She opened it and crept in. Oculis realised that there was someone in there, and she knew exactly who it was. Carefully, Elisia sat on a bench in the church, Oculis instructed Argent to stay with Elisia. Oculis sped down a thin corridor, lead by her sisters to an equally as thin door right at the other side of the hallway. She opened it and crept in.

Gemini had heard them come in, he hadn't stuck around to see who it was. Instead, he had hid behind a bed in one of the rooms. It was a bit dusty, but he wasn't complaining. He just didn't want to be back in that castle.

He thought the church was safe, he smacked himself in the head at his own stupidity, the guards probably knew all about it. He buried his face in his hands as someone opened the door.

"Gemini?" They said.

He didn't know who they were, but somehow they knew him. He awkwardly stood up as slow as he could.

"Don't be afraid, I'm Oculis."

He stepped out from where he was hiding and almost fell over a box in his way, she laughed at this. He gave a weak smile. "I don't need to introduce myself, you know my name." He paused. "So, I've got a few questions, how do you know my name? How did you find me? And who else is with you?"

She sensed his care for Elisia almost immediately, it was in his smile.

"I have Elisia with me." She said.

He kept his head down and tried to conceal his relief, "Where?"

"The main bit of the church, she's a little battered up but …" Her voice tailed off as he burst out the door and thundered down into the main church area.

"Elisia!" He called, he bashed open the giant doors and saw two people on a bench. One was Elisia, and the other was a guy who had a sword. The guy instantly put it up in defence, luckily Oculis appeared and told him what was going on.

He nodded and reluctantly put it down, instead stared at Gemini.

If he was honest it was a tad uncomfortable.

"What are you looking at?" he said throatily.

The guy didn't seem to care, he just sat back down and closed his eyes.

Gemini slowly came closer to the bench, and as soon as he saw her arm and ankle, he went even slower as dread filled his mind.

"That's a catacomb bite." He said, and turned to Oculis.

"Yeah, I'm still not sure how it happened. These two won't tell me." She replied, still standing in the doorway, arms folded.

Argent snapped open his eyes and got up quickly, grabbing his sword as he went. "I heard a scattering noise." He whispered.

Gemini sat himself down on the bench by Elisia, she was sweating, clearly the dream she was having was awful. Stupid Night Childs, he went to wake her but a hand stopped him. "I wouldn't do that, the nightmare will stay with her for the rest of her life if you wake her up."

He looked up at Oculis. This was the first chance he'd had to see her properly, and if he as honest she was the most beautiful thing he had ever set his eyes on. She seemed to notice him staring in amazement.

"I'm half ink angel," She explained, "I'm not going to turn you into one, it's only a full ink angel that can do that."

"Oh." He said, then he returned to Elisia. "Can her wounds be healed by you, then?"

Oculis bent down and inspected the wounds, "Yes, but they will leave scars."

Elisia moaned in her sleep.

"If I know Elisia, she'll love scars." Gemini said lovingly.

Argent looked at the doors, sword pointed at them.

"I can heal them now; just don't blame me if she doesn't like them." Oculis said.

Gemini watched as black inky silk fell from the half ink angel's finger tips; the silk wrapped itself round the wounds. And then, as if nothing had happened, the silk disappeared and all that was left was a light scar on Elisia's arm and ankle.

Immediately, Elisia awoke and sat up, inspected her scars and smiled.

"These look brilliant," She said. At this, well Gemini could only smile.

Oculis turned her attention to Argent, he hadn't said much since he had pointed his sword at the doors. She concentrated her attention on his mind, and suddenly a memory flashed before her eyes.

"**Move!**" A younger version of Argent yelled at the people, he threw his sword at the doors and perfectly barricaded them. But this was not enough.

The people inside screamed as the windows smashed open and guards began pouring in and seizing people, witches, babies, spies. Argent ran forward and pulled his sword out of the door, staggering over backwards in the process. "**Son!**"

Argent turned to see his father seized by one of the guards.

"**Dad**!" He cried out, but one of the guards almost caught him as he ran towards his father. "**Run away from here!**" His father yelled at him, "**Run!**"

Argent's face had a tear roll down it as he burst the doors open and ran for his life.

Oculis came back to her own mind and looked at the quiet Argent with sympathy, she didn't offer him a hug or offer to a talk, she knew that even though Argent wanted one, he wouldn't let himself.

So, instead, as she went past she put a hand on his shoulder, he looked up in surprise and she gave him a nod as she left him to his thoughts.

*****

The next day was good for Elisia, she had no pains, no aches, and no nightmares. They ate well as Oculis had bought all the food they had had from camp, all in all it was a good start to the day.

Elisia was sitting next to Oculis discussing what to do next.

"Both my parents are dead, I know my father must be, and a ghost outside this temple told me that my mother is." Elisia said.

"That ghost was lying, they can do that you know." Oculis replied stubbornly.

"So, she's alive?" she said, hopeful.

"I don't know, but that ghost wouldn't have known either."

There was no time for smiles and laughs, or to even take in the news, as Argent and Gemini burst in the doors in panic.

Elisia immediately rose as news hit her ears.

The recent friction between Timki and Annika had developed, into war. All worlds had taken a side, that means all worlds were about to be hit by war. Including this one.

"We need to get out of here!" Elisia yelled panic stricken. She grabbed her cloak (which Oculis had picked up and placed in her bag when taking everything from the camp) and headed out the door.

She was quickly followed by Argent, Gemini and Oculis.

They walked hurriedly into the cover of the forest, in the very deep depths of the wood, they stopped to rest. Breathing heavily, Elisia leaned up against a tree and bent down with her hands on her knees.

"What's the war over?" She said finally, to end the panicked silence.

"We don't know, we just saw a couple of groups of people who explained the situation." Gemini said, looking at Argent.

Argent nodded, "They only said something about some locket. I think Timki accuses Annika of having it, but Annika insists that they don't."

Gemini added, "I thought it was over some bloody land. But apparently it was just a cover from what was really going on …"

The word locket jumped up in Elisia's head, she looked at Oculis. Oculis already knew.

"Elisia, I think it's time you explained something **important**." She said roughly.

Elisia breathed, "Alright … fine …" she hesitated. "Ages ago, I was sneaking around in Kerkavia's room when she came in with someone else … I only had time to quickly hide under the bed, Marcellus came in and gave her a fake locket, and then he asked me to come out of my hiding place. He told me of a legend, a legend of …"

"The Bellum Locket? Everyone's heard that." Argent interrupted.

Elisia hurried on "He had the locket, he wouldn't let me see it. And then he went strange, he went mad. I didn't know what to do, so I just ran off."

Everyone was silent for a minute.

"There was someone else in the room with you Elisia, and it was the only person who knows more about the locket than you do." Whispered Oculis, her eyes at the floor.

"Who?" Argent asked.

Elisia looked at Oculis's sudden reluctance, then realised.

"You Oculis, you have it don't you? You stole it from him ..."

It all started to fall into place.

"Your ink angels called my name, your ink angels told me an oracle. You stole it, so I could throw it over the edge."

Oculis nodded.

"There's one problem. As soon as you throw it over the edge, all the souls it's touched will deform and twist." Oculis whispered.

For the first time ever, Elisia saw fear in Oculis's eyes.

But it had to be done.

Chapter Eighteen

On The Run

They had all decided to camp for the night, Argent was sharpening his sword with a bit of flint he'd taken from the church wall, Oculis was in her tent, and Gemini was sitting next to Elisia chucking another log on the fire. The sparks flew up, causing the fire to crackle and heave.

"Oh, and I kind of forgot to mention something else …" Gemini said, looking at the fire. "Your … um … kind of… …" He sighed, "Your wanted for questioning."

"**What**?" Elisia stood up in fury, "**Why have you failed to tell me this**?!"

"I didn't think it mattered that much," Gemini shrugged his shoulders, "Sorry."

Elisia slumped down on the floor.

Argent looked up as she did so, "It could be worse, there's always a silver lining to a cloud." He smiled at her, and she tried her best to give a convincing smile back.

Gemini got up to go in his tent after a while, (the one amazing thing about spells is that you can make anything with them) Elisia, however, got up and claimed she was going for a walk.

"Then I'm coming with you." Argent announced, to which Elisia shrugged her shoulders. They both walked in silence for a minute, the young witch was looking at the scars on her arm, as if reminding herself not to stray into dangerous zones.

"What are you going to do?" He whispered, stopping where he was.

But Elisia couldn't hear him; she could see something in the forest, quite far away. Soundlessly, she pointed towards it, Argent nodded. Keeping low, she made her way towards the bright object with Argent following in her wake.

As soon as they came close, they saw many white blurs crowded near a tree.

"They're spirits ..." Whispered Elisia as quiet as she could. She peered over the edge of the fallen tree they had crouched behind, they all looked so frightened. Argent peered over in concern, obviously he was wondering what would scare a spirit.

That answer came sooner than expected. Out of the nearby trees, Sials came from near and far, surrounding the spirits. Elisia grabbed Argent's arm, "this is their hunt." Argent looked at Elisia with question in his eyes, and went back to watching.

All at once the Sials plunged forwards, high pitched screams and wails threatened to blow the nearby trees over. Despair exploded outwards, it filled Elisia's ears and senses until she was shaking. Elisia looked back, as if watching the scream echo throughout the forest. Reluctantly, she looked back at the Sials, but they had gone; as well as the spirits.

Argent got up slowly, and helped Elisia up. He seemed to notice her despair to help. "Elisia, there was nothing you could of done. Sials are creatures of the dark, that's how they feed. It's the circle of life."

"I know, but it's still kind of sad." She replied.

He nodded, and they walked back in silence.

*****

"Get up! Elisia please get up! Damn! Wake up!"
Elisia awoke to someone shaking her shoulders, she opened her eyes "arugh, what ..."

"Someone saw us in the forest! They're going to alert the guards!" Elisia looked up to see Gemini's panic stricken face staring down at her in worry, "we need to get up and move!"

Elisia immediately got up and seized her bag; ran out of her tent, waved her hand and the tent disappeared.

"Where too?" She said, standing in the middle of the hustle and bustle of things.

"Just go, with Argent, ahead of us, we'll catch up!" Oculis urged, "Just go!".

Elisia hurried forward to where Argent was waiting, he smiled. "C'mon then!" He said, running ahead of her. Elisia smiled, the worst mistake anyone can make is trying to out run her.

She picked up her pace, making sure she kept in time to her counting, and sure enough, Argent was soon left behind. Laughing to herself, she slowed to get her breath back.

Eventually he caught up and laughed in amazement, "Your one tough cookie to beat," he paused, "at running." He breathed and gave her a toothy grin.

They both walked for a bit, Elisia noticed that after a while the forest was thinning. She voiced this concern to Argent.

He looked around, "I hadn't, but I do now. I reckon we should turn around ..." suddenly, a ton of voices sped themselves around them, Elisia was grabbed and pulled closer to Argent by Argent himself.

"What are they?" She whispered, she was surprised her whisper was heard above all the noise. But even so, Argent didn't answer her. His eyes were darting all over the forest, obviously he was looking for a way out.

"Two little children walking round the woods, one fell down and the other one died."

Elisia turned around in wonder, she saw a witch standing where the voice came from. She was wearing a plain black dress, cobwebs covered her hair thinly, and spiders crawled over her hands. Elisia took a step back, but Argent took a step forward.

"Who are you?" He demanded to know, sword raised.

The witch seemed fearless at the sharp metal object pointing towards her, until she took a closer look at it.

"I ... I'm Tympeli Callous ... a witch! Look I'm harmless, put that away!" She pleaded.

Argent peered at his sword and smiled. "I'll spare your life if you let us go."

"Yes! Yes!" She nodded many times, and pointed to an opening in the wall of voices. "Just don't hurt me!"

Don't hurt her? Argent isn't like that … is he? Argent came over and grabbed Elisia's arm, the grip was firm but comfortable, and walked her over to the gap, the whole time keeping his sword pointed on the witch. Who looked back at him in deep fear …

Once safely clear of the witch's web of voices, Elisia looked at Argent, he hadn't looked at her since the incident.

"What is that sword?" Elisia whispered.

He stopped, and turned to her and stared her straight in the eye. "I'm not dangerous, ok? It's just a sword." He tilted his head and sighed, then got the sword out. "The devils revenge …" He stared at it for a moment then placed it back in his belt.

Elisia didn't say anything, she just started walking again. Devil's revenge? Sounds like a fairy tale.

Oculis and Gemini eventually caught up with them, and as usual, Oculis noticed the silence between them as soon as she came close. But luckily, she didn't sense what it was about.

Later, when they had made another camp (being more careful to keep everything in their bags in case they had to run off again) Elisia dared to ask Gemini a question that had been bugging her.

"Gem," she whispered, "What is the devil's revenge?"

He looked at her in surprise, "Why the hell would you want to know about that? It's this old campfire story,"

"We are at a campfire." Elisia said shrugging.

"Well," He said, looking at her and scratching his head.

"Alright then, just don't go have nightmares. Waking you up this morning at half six was bad enough, I don't want to have to get up and shake you awake because of a nightmare too." He sighed and looked at the fire, "Basically, it's a classic tale of a man wanting a sword, so he makes a fire out of various body parts of people he's killed and creates a sword out of the flames. The sword contains the power to kill

138

anyone, anywhere. For example, there was a case a few years ago of this bloody bastard just suddenly dropping dead at his house. Witches couldn't find anything wrong with him except a burn on his neck, in the shape of the devils eye."

Elisia looked at him in silent shock for a minute, and then mumbled in thanks. Part of her wish she hadn't asked.

*****

Tenebrae's fox form was streaking across the wooden floor of the bar, no one had seen him; yet. He knew he would be caught eventually; he just had to find the object he was looking for.

Marcellus was in his room, dying apparently. Tenebrae smiled, it was nice to know the old idiot was going back where he came from: Hell.

Streaking quietly into the room, he checked the unconscious man's neck, pockets and bed. Wasn't there.

"Damn." He whispered.

Footsteps started pounding up the stairs, the old man groaned; Tenebrae looked around the room for a way out. A window.

As quietly as he came, he slipped away, uncaught.

But now he knew for sure, she had it. Dread filled his body – her sanity it was going to die.

*****

Oculis awoke with tears streaming down her face; she wiped them away calmly, unzipped her tent, and went walking.

After a while she stopped far enough for the camp not to hear her. She spoke softly, and out of her finger there formed a tiger made from the darkest ink. It gazed at her, and then it streaked off into the distance to Tenebrae: it was time she told him the truth. She listened for a few moments, and went back to camp.

The next morning was tiring, they got up earlier than usual to avoid staying in one place for long. Gemini was not a cheerful chappy, he liked his lie-in's. Swearing as he got up, he gathered his things and waved his tent away, it didn't go. He tried it again, and it didn't go, the same thing happened five times before it actually decided to go.

"Do you always have trouble like that?" Oculis said, concerned.

"I'm not good at magic." He shrugged his shoulders.

"Try using your wrist a bit more; trust me." She replied as they made their way out of camp with Elisia and Argent following sleepily, "They're so tired," she whispered, nudging Gemini. He turned and nodded.

"So, Gemini," Oculis said, "Who are you in Elisia's life?".

"Well," he began, yawning and looking away from Oculis for a minute, "I'm not really sure, I know I have a pair of set boots in her life, but I don't know where those boots are, if you understand."

She nodded, urging him to continue with her interested eyes.

"Ever since she was young, I've always been around. She's always loved my shop, we used to sit by the fire with a cup of tea chatting about the day. Sometimes we'd go in the forest looking for an adventure, but there was no need, it always found us. At first, it was fun and games, but then bad stuff started happening, I almost lost her once …" He faded out as his mind weaved in and out of memories.

"What happened?" She whispered, cautiously. As if she was worried she was intruding on his memories.

He shook his head, "It was awful. We went down to the river on a stormy day, she found a piece of moonstone and we were heading back, chatting, laughing … Elisia suddenly fell down beside me, at first I thought she was joking, but then I panicked … I remember turning her over and holding her, the expression on her face was peaceful yet … I hated it. The moonstone eventually fell out of her hand and she started twitching. It clicked. I was intelligent enough to realise the moonstone she had found was cursed, so I threw it back in the river carefully avoiding touching it. She eventually came round, after I carried her home and put her to bed … still … she woke up after a while, and all I remember her saying was

'Gem, why can't I remember anything? All I remember is screaming …' I got her to sleep eventually … but it was ok. It was just another adventure." He fell silent.

Nobody talked after that, not for hours. It seemed like the whole world was silently waiting for a new page to be turned, but nobody would turn it.

Chapter Nineteen

The Gate Keeper

$\mathcal{F}$ ive straight hours of silence held them all, Elisia and Argent seemed too tired to speak, Oculis was thinking about what Gemini had said, and Gemini was lost in his memories.

This all came to a sudden halt when they saw the gate.

The gate was five times taller than Elisia. It was made of black iron, and each streak of it curved and danced gracefully. It was almost like it had a mind of its own.

Elisia immediately straightened her back in interest,

"Where are we? What is this?" She whispered, coming closer to Gemini.

"I'm not sure," he replied.

Oculis shook her head, "I didn't think we'd come this far already ... this doesn't make sense."

Elisia took a cautious step forward as everyone was looking at Oculis staring at her map with confusion; although Elisia couldn't see it clearly, she just about managed to figure out why she couldn't understand the wording above the iron.

"It's in Romanian."

Latin was the language of magic, but it was originally Romanian, 100,000 years ago that is. Why would something as old as this not be knocked down already?

She took another step forward after announcing the language, and the iron in the gate seemed to notice her. Within seconds, it had spelled out her whole name.

Oculis looked up and with caution, took one step forward towards Elisia, slotting away her map. "Elisia, that gate, it's the Dragon's gate."

"Dragon's gate?" Elisia questioned, keeping a careful eye on the iron's movements.

She saw Oculis nod at her from the corner of her eye, "Ask to be let in, it will present you with a question, if you get it incorrect, you die."

Argent and Gemini immediately opened their mouths to object, but Oculis silenced them with her hand. Part of Elisia wished they had objected anyway, what if it asked something she didn't know? What if it was maths? Was there a time limit on how long you had to answer?

"Um ..." Elisia began, talking to the gate. "Can I come in?"

The iron didn't move for a moment, and then with many creaks and squeaks it began turning into a question. Within seconds again, the question was presented. It was: where is the devil's revenge?

Oculis was silent for a moment, and then she spoke with a calm voice "Elisia it will only ask a question it knows you know ..."

Elisia stood silent for a moment, trying to figure out what an earth she should do. If she said the answer, it would mean Argent would be feared by everyone, people would probably kill him to get the sword. So he could possibly die.

But if she didn't say it, she would definitely die.

Elisia heard the clang of Argents sword, he'd made it appear, and he was holding it in his capable hands. "Don't worry about me Elisia, just say the truth." He told her.

What if there was a time limit on how long you had to answer?

"The sword is ..." She gulped, it's now or never, "The devil's revenge is in Argent's hands!"

Gemini took a step back from Argent in shock and fear, his mouth was open as if he was about to yell at Argent, but no words came. Gemini was speechless.

The gate made no movement for a few seconds, and then the iron weaved out of the way, letting the gate clearly swing open.

Everyone stood silent for a moment; Elisia's nerves were causing her to shake. How close had she come to death? Oculis started walking towards the gate, giving Elisia an encouraging nod. Argent strayed behind as they began walking in, he didn't even come close when Elisia gestured him to …

The giant stone path looked burnt, plus it was hovering a few inches off the ground. There was no green grass, just burnt dead grass, with broken statues lying around them equally as burnt. Oculis used her magic to fix them, when Elisia looked at her questionably; she said "he likes breaking them."

At the end of the pathway, there was a ruined castle. The roof was full of holes, the bricks were broken in two, some of the walls were lumbering in on the rooms, leaving the inside exposed for all to see … but they didn't walk all the way. Instead they stopped in sight of it, while Oculis yelled "Cutaz!"

The ground shook and a giant roar echoed over the grounds, Argent immediately pushed forward and raised his sword high in defence as the dragon appeared.

Violet and green scales covered its giant structure, its wings cut through the air gracefully, and as it landed, Elisia saw his eyes were silver, with big black pupils.

"Oculis," Cutaz spoke in a low rough tone, "You called woman?"

"Woman?" She questioned, crossing her arms, clearly offended. "Shall I start ignoring your name and call you dragon, Cutaz?"

He ignored her last comment and looked towards Argent.

"Sword bearer put that down …" He peered closer at the sword, his giant eyes narrowing in focus. "Oh wait, you are the devil's revenge bearer. You are a young one, drunk with fearlessness."

Argent dropped his guard and looked at the dragon with raised eyebrows.

"Elisia Ivy Crewman," the dragon said, "We have much to discuss child, but you are not a child, your mind is stretched through experience, you are nothing like a child."

Elisia didn't know what to say to this, so she just stood there in silence.

Cutaz turned towards Gemini, "Hmmm, I sense much pain and sorrow within this one. You're much a tortured soul, are you not?"

Gemini took a step towards Elisia and pushed her back behind him.

"Ah," Cutaz whispered, yet, his whisper echoed for miles. "You are protective, yet scared of your own shadow? You are most puzzling, master Gemini … come, my castle awaits your arrival."

Tenebrae had spent days on foot; he was following the trail of the Ink Tiger Oculis had left behind for him. She obviously didn't intend for him to follow it, but he'd managed to cast a spell on it before it had finished giving its message, and now he was hot on her heels.

The final push would be to get through the gate of the dragon … that would be hard. Considering the dragon hated his guts because Tenebrae was the one who chained the beast there in the first place.

But he had to get to the locket; he had to get it off her before the fate sunk in. She'd only had it for a few months; it takes half a year for it to sink in. That's one hundred and eighty-two days, and he'd had one hundred and seventy-three of them already. She couldn't die; it meant she would turn into a full ink angel and completely forget everyone. She would be reborn.

He would leave straight away, after he'd got the locket.

He approached the gate with caution.

*****

146

Elisia loved the castle, but the dragon had given her a job, to go down to the gate. She didn't really see why, but as soon as she saw Tenebrae on the other side she ran towards the gate, just as his question was presented.

*****

Is Elisia your daughter?

*****

Tenebrae stood for a moment, he had to answer honestly, despite the person on the other side of the gate.

"Yes." He said.

Immediately the iron in the gate began to move and creak, just as it swung open, he saw Elisia look at him in shock.

Oh shit.

*****

Elisia turned on her heels.

"Elisia!" He shouted and ran after her, "Let me explain!"

She whipped around.

He stopped in his tracks.

She stared at him, and he stared back. They both refused to break the gaze, both refused to back down; both refused to let their blood relative walk away without hearing them out. Elisia's face flashed with fury and she stepped determinedly forwards; she felt disgusted, lied too. Her skin was crawling at the sight of him, the liar. The one man she had come all this way to search for, and here he was, he wasn't heroic, wasn't noble.

Just a liar.

"You ..." She spat, "You are **no** blood relative of mine."

Angry tears formed in her eyes as she ripped the gaze apart, and turned away from him. Disappointment smashed down on her mind, anger seizing her soul and ripping it up. All she could hear is the ripping, the sound of the tare, the break. She could see nothing but a blurred path underneath her feet.

Yet, behind her was someone to blame, someone she could take it out on reasonably ... someone, she could smash into pieces and have an excuse, a reason for violence. Behind her, there was someone she could hurt and be cured from this vile disgust.

Yet, she did not.

His temper rose in frustration of her audacity to walk away, "Do not speak to me like that!" He yelled across the courtyard.

He watched her keep walking.

"I am your father!" He yelled in an angry desperate tone, "and I tell you to turn around right **now**!"

She whipped around again, sending rocks bouncing across the ground.

"*Trădătorii trebuie să fie pedepsiți.*"

The words poured out of Elisia's mouth uncontrollably, along with anger and a taste for revenge.

A dark whirl wind caught his mind in its claws and squeezed until he could not resist it.

Elisia's screams as a child filled his ears so he could hear nothing else, Elisia's pain clutched his heart and clawed at it, leaving marks. Her near death experiences were shoved in front of his eyes, her tears filled his own, making everything blurred … emotions, thoughts, screams … everything piled onto his shoulders. He shook and slammed his palms into his head, as if trying to knock the hold off. It would not budge. He collapsed to his knees, shaking and screaming, whining and hurting. He held his head in his hands, hearing the screams of his daughter he could have stopped.

"No more!" He managed to whisper through shaking lips, tears streamed down his face. He tried to shut his eyes, to shut it out, but more memories forced themselves into his mind and his eyes opened suddenly, and he stared on in Elisia's direction.

A wave of guilt threw itself at her and she blinked and panicked. A sudden realisiation at what she had done through itself at her.

A thump next to Elisia made her turn; Cutaz had gracefully landed next to her and now whispered, "That's quite enough Elisia."

"What do I do? How do I stop it!"

"Say Lumina."

"Lumina ..."

The black claw let go, and the screams halted, the memories stopped ... and he was left back with his own messed up emotions, and wounds from Elisia's. Deep wounds.

Shakily, he staggered up ... but fell onto the rocks breathing heavily.

Elisia rushed forward to help, but was stopped by Cutaz.

"He'll be fine," Cutaz said through clenched teeth, "He always is."

The young witch looked at her hands in disgust at what she had done, "What happened to me ..."

"You unlocked the power you were always meant to have, come with me."

With a simple hover charm, Elisia managed to transport Tenebrae and herself into a room in the castle. The young witch quickly slipped her father onto the single bed in the corner, he still looked awful, but part of her had lost care for him.

The room was beautiful; the windows spread light all over the library, so many books, so many bindings and covers. But the best thing about them is that they were magic books.

Cutaz stuck his head through the hole in the ceiling and instructed Elisia to grab the biggest book from the top shelf then climb up to the roof.

Elisia immediately grabbed the book, "it's heavy!" she exclaimed, and pushed it up to the dragon ... well, she tried to. It ended up slipping back down and hitting her head with a loud, throbbing thud.

Elisia used various charms to get it to go into the right direction, and then she followed.

Once up on the roof, Elisia got a good look at the book. It was gorgeous; the front cover was pure white, with a circular orb full of mist in the centre. Elisia touched it, and it reacted to her touch, the mist instantly following her fingers. She circled round in delight, and then opened the book with care. Each page was golden and thin, yet you couldn't rip them.

"It's brilliant."

The dragon smiled at her, "turn to the one-hundredth page."

Elisia carefully turned the pages until she met the right one, she placed it down and peered over it to have a look.

"Read it out." Cutaz ordered.

> "Within a dark age,
> A dark evil will rise.
> Below them, a feud,
> But with guns and knives.
> A baby, but mind,
> No baby like any other,
> Without father or mother.
> And she will grow,
> She'll bring back the tongues,
> Of 100,000 years of lost ones.
> With angels to guide her alone,
> To home.
> She'll crack open the bellum,
> With dead skin and bone."

Elisia fell silent for a moment.

"It's about me?" She finally managed to say.

"Indeed, I cannot explain too much as it is a prophecy, but keep the book, it will be as light as air once you pick it up, as it does not have much knowledge of you yet ... oh, and Oculis and Argent are down the stairs in the dining room, if you feel like joining them you may, but I strongly urge you let Tenebrae explain first before you go telling everyone. You owe him that much, young one." And with that, Cutaz flew off, leaving Elisia to her thoughts.

Eventually, Elisia climbed down from the roof and back into the library, moving a few bricks out of the way so she could get through to a rocking chair in the corner of the room, and there she sat, rocking back and forth, looking at Tenebrae and then the floor.

The chair rocked back and forth.

Why not tell her? Where had he got the scar on his eye from? Does he know where Mirum is? Did he cheat on Mirum with Oculis? Does Oculis have any idea who he really is? Did he change his name? Will he give her any answers anyway?

Elisia sat rocking for hours, staring at the floor, it was only when Tenebrae awoke and saw her did she pull out of her mind set. She didn't say a word though, she was too worn out for that.

"Elisia, I can explain ..." He began, sitting up and looking at her on the bed. "Me and your mother ... I met her when I was only young, in those days I was a proper trained assassin, I was ... I was convinced I couldn't have her when I was so dangerous myself ... so I fled to do some protection on Oculis's father, but he was killed right in front of me ... I couldn't get over the guilt even when I returned home the guilt still lingered ... and when your mother saw what they had done to me she told me to quit, to change my name and settle down ... it was hard, but I did it eventually." He sighed, "They found me after four years of hiding, you were only two then, but they attacked you with knives ... you have a light scar on your right arm from it ..." Elisia looked at her arm, a small but loud scar clung to her arm. He was right. "They told me they would get you again unless I went looking for the bellum locket, I thought it would only take a few days ... but it didn't ... your mother came after me ... and ... and she ..." he gulped as a small tear slid from his eye, "she was killed by a fire caused by a dragon on the loose, she almost made it out ... but they ... they ... they shoved her into it again ... I couldn't do ..."

He moaned as he clasped his head as ache threatened to tear it apart, "I was convinced I was a bad luck charm for all of you, so I never came back ..."

Elisia stopped rocking.

"That spell as really damaged your emotions, hasn't it?" She said, with a shaking voice.

151

He reluctantly nodded, "I'm so sorry for leaving you all them years, but it was for your own good, do you understand?"

She nodded, and bit her lip as he tried to stand but couldn't.

"Maybe there's something I can do to help you ..." she stood up and focused her mind. Suddenly she snapped open her eyes, flames danced behind them and she placed a hand on Tenebrae's head *"spiritul de vindecare!"*

Tenebrae felt like a sharp needle was stitching up his broken mind, the room became ten times clearer, the room, the book on Elisia's chair, and Argent lingering in the door way, with a concerned expression on his face. The pain suddenly disappeared and Elisia turned towards Argent.

"We need you down stairs Tenebrae, something's happened to Oculis."

He immediately rose up with panic in his bones.

The room was big enough to fit two dragons in comfortably, and in the centre was a small rectangular table. The ceiling was pure white and the walls were grey stone, but surprisingly the floor was wood. Oculis was sitting in the centre with a dazed look in her eye.

"Oculis?" Said Tenebrae in a low voice, but it still echoed all around the room. She didn't answer.

Carefully, he took the locket off her neck and stared at it for a moment.

"Elisia, I'm doing this for you."

"What?"

He went to put the locket on his neck but was shot back by Elisia's magic, and he dropped it.

"I won't let you."

He scrambled up and stayed back, "Elisia, you don't understand ... it has to be in someone's hands or it will ... it will ..."

Cutaz interrupted "If I may be so bold, the locket is safe here not worn by anyone. No one is able to get through here unless they open the gate, and I am aware of anyone who comes near the gate."

152

Oculis seemed to be coming round.

"Cutaz, can you put a protection spell on it? So no one can pick it up except when its needed ?" Tenebrae said.

The dragon nodded and closed his eyes, a golden globe of protection suddenly appeared over the locket.

Oculis got up, "what happened? I was holding the locket and then I just heard ..."

"Don't worry, its sorted," Said Argent, sitting at the table rather angrily.

Tenebrae walked out of the room after Oculis mentioned Gemini, someone he hadn't met before. Oculis had followed, and the dragon had flown off to destroy some statues, so Elisia and Argent were alone.

"You don't seem yourself." Elisia announced, kicking off her boots and making a wash bowl appear in front of her. She dipped her face in and let down her dark black hair from its plait, then twisted out all the access water (to prevent her hair from dripping all over the floor) and dipped her boots in to wash them.

"I'm not," He replied, looking at the table. "I just feel like I don't belong here."

Elisia stopped dipping her boots in and out of the water and took her jacket off, "nobody really belongs anywhere, I don't really belong here. I belong out in the forest finding new kinds of berries or something ..."

He briefly smiled, "could you make a mirror and wash bowl for me like that?" he looked at her, interested.

She clicked her fingers twice, and a wash bowl and mirror appeared near him.

Elisia clicked her fingers again and made a screen for herself, and one for him. He peered round at her in confusion.

"I'm going to get changed ..." she explained, to which he suddenly nodded and hid back behind the screen.

Elisia created two outfits before she found the one she liked, a dark green knee length dress with black leggings and blue boots. She changed into them and made her other clothes disappear with a flick of her hand, she removed her screen and wash bowl, took off her boots and started humming and dancing around bare footed.

She did a ballerina like twirl then went bright red in embarrassment; Argent had got rid of his screen, washbowl and mirror and was watching her.

"Can you dance?" He questioned, raising his eyebrows.

"A bit," Elisia replied, still looking at the floor.

He smiled at her embarrassment, "show me."

Elisia raised around her head for an excuse, "there's no music ..."

Just as she said that Oculis started playing a piano in another room.

A giant grin had placed itself on Argent's face, "now there is."

Realising she literally had no choice, she took herself to the other side of the hall and waited for the right moment to start. Gracefully, she begun, she did a cartwheel and landed perfectly. On her tippy toes lunged into a twirl and landed with legs bent. Lifting her head up, she let her body take control. She moved with the music, let it control her every limb until she was almost a puppet. She didn't have to think about it anymore, she just did what she wanted. She felt almost as if she was skating on ice, and as the last note was played she crossed her legs and sat on the floor with her head low.

Argent clapped, "your pretty damn good." A smile appeared on his face and the music begun again, "but I'm more into fighting," he put his guard up and pretended to punch her; she caught his fist and smiled. "You made me dance; now it's your turn."

His smiled immediately disappeared.

Her hand still closed tightly on his fist, she made him twirl round.

"Not so funny now is it?" She whispered.

A smirk appeared on Argents face and he pulled Elisia close to him, "Do you waltz madam?"

She shoved away from him, "You brat!"

He started running away from her and she chased him, they did three laps around the room before he got tired and surrendered to her, "Alright! Alright! I'll dance, I'll dance!" he breathed, just as Gemini walked in.

Elisia helped him up, swearing she would get her revenge.

Elisia was glad to collapse into the bed in the library. Her brain was aching from the amount of information she'd had to force into it today, and although she didn't like sleep because of her nightmares, this time she was just glad to be able to close her eyes.

Close her eyes, not sleep.

She considered waking the dragon up, but wasn't that very rude? Couldn't she 'accidently' drop a giant book so it makes a big noise and wakes him up anyway? No, surely the dragon would know.

Her mother said in her diary that reading was the key to sleeping, so, she took out the book the great dragon had given her. He was right; the book had become much lighter now. Then again, she shouldn't be so surprised, dragons were known for being wise creatures.

"I suppose we are," Said a voice above her.

She looked up to see Cutaz staring down through the hole in the roof.

"I'm sorry! I didn't mean to wake you." She whispered at him, and that was the truth, she had been careful to hardly make a sound.

"It was your whirling mind that woke me, child. Why are you not sleeping?"

"I don't like sleep ..." Elisia shamefully said.

"Ah, scared of the old night child are you?" He said roughly, laughing a little.

"The what?"

"The night child, oh, tell me you have heard about them! They bring nightmares, nothing to be afraid of. They are cowardly, cowardly beings that use harmless dreams to try and hurt you." Cutaz closed his eyes while speaking to Elisia, this made the young witch feel guilty for waking him.

"Is there a way to keep them out?" Elisia whispered.

The dragon sighed, "I am afraid not, you puzzle me Elisia, you are so scared of the silliest things …"

The dragon pulled a scale off himself, the place where it had been had started to bleed green blood, and passed it to Elisia with magic.

"Keep it, if you ever need me, I will know."

Elisia looked up at the dragon gratefully, "Thank you, Cutaz is there anything I can do for you?"

He looked at her for a moment, then pulled his head out of the hole in the roof, and said "Yes, my child, stop thinking so much and sleep."

Elisia smiled to herself, clasped the scale in her hand, closed her eyes and whispered "Goodnight Cutaz."

But no reply came.

*****

Elisia awoke from sleep calmly without suddenly being shaken awake, without suddenly being alert, without any of the usual panic she had when she opened her eyes. For once, she was peacefully awake. She smiled to herself, for the first time in months; she can lie in without anyone needing her up. She sat up slowly, her night gown sleepily sliding off the bed as she swung her legs over the edge and placed her feet on to the stone floor. She smiled. It was extremely cold.

Elisia looked down at the dark green and purple scale in her hand. It was actually rather big (about the size of a baby's clenched fist), it was a quite thick, and a pointed oval shape. She used magic to make a small bit of red string and drilled a small hole in the side of the scale, and threaded the string through and placed it round her neck.

It seemed to shimmer as she got up and started doing her usual morning routine, bath, brush of teeth, change of clothes, wash the others … the list could go on for hours, and sometimes it did. This morning was not like that though, this morning she was done and dusted in under half an hour (with the help of good old fashioned magic).

Her boots tapped on the stone steps as she made her way down to the dining room, looking for everyone. Shouldn't they all be up by now? It was half seven. Perhaps they are all enjoying the lie in, like she was earlier.

"Elisia …"

She turned on the last step. Had she imagined it?

"Elisia…"

No, that was definitely real. She recognised the voice, but she didn't know who it belonged to.

"Elisia…"

Scared, yet interested, she walked towards the call. It lead her exactly where she was heading; the dining room.

Elisia carefully slid open the door and crept inside, looking for the source of the noise.

"Hello?" She whispered.

"Hello." It replied.

She couldn't find the source, mostly because it seemed to be the room speaking to her.

"To whom am I speaking?" She whispered again in confusion, turning all around the room still looking for a mouth of some sort.

"You are not speaking to whom; you are speaking to a room." It echoed back to her ears.

"Well … I've never really done this before." Elisia said, deciding to stand still and just speak. She clearly wasn't going to find anything to look at.

"Of course you have not. You've only recently just got your powers, and that dragon scale you've got gives you the knowledge all hours," the room said.

"Tell me, room, do you always talk in rhyme?" Elisia stubbornly replied.

A noise from behind her made her whip round in shock, until she realised who it was.

"Cutaz, you shouldn't sneak up on me like that!" She snapped at him, worried that he might of heard her randomly chatting to a room.

"I forgot to mention something important, come outside. I cannot really fit in here." The great dragon calmly spoke to her, completely oblivious to her embarrassment.

Carefully climbing out a window, she landed on burnt grass, rather soft stuff.

"Now, Elisia ..." He began, settling himself down and looking at her with wide eyes. "I should have told you this the first moment I had, but other things crossed my mind. You have the rare gift of speaking Romanian, the old language of magic ..."

Elisia nodded.

"100,000 years ago the magic of the lands were united, together. There was no witch world or demon world; there was just one world that contained both magical and non-magical people. You would have known this if you had bothered to look in the book ... both witches and wizards alike would work in peace and harmony with non-magical women and men ... even magical creatures could roam the lands without being hunted." He rolled his eyes as Elisia made a hand gesture which meant 'get to the point'.

"Romanian people of the old world had a belief, and that belief meant that everything natural, everything that could speak and could not, had a spirit within it. And they had the power to awaken such spirits and bring them to life."

Elisia opened her mouth to question, but he silenced her.

"The non-magical humans of the world did not agree in such beliefs, and when they began cutting down trees and killing animals, a war began between the two people. Ripping the world apart, conflicts killed thousands of witches and wizards, as well as hundreds of thousands of humans."

Elisia fell extremely silent, everything seemed to follow her in it. No birds would sing, no wind would glide through objects calmly, it was as if everything in the whole entire world was holding its breathe.

"You and my scale combined have increased your powers tremendously. You can now awaken those spirits without meaning to, so I must ask you humbly to be careful Elisia, and stay clear of that locket. If you wake it without meaning too, all hell will break loose. I suppose I could take it off you, but you will require it in your life." He lowered his voice so it was a whisper, "be wary Elisia, be very wary ... those close but far away are the ones that will attempt to kill you. Time and time … again."

Chapter Twenty

You Always Leave Me

The dragon's warnings had sent Elisia far away from the dining room over the last three days, Oculis knew why probably better than anyone else, and frankly she was worried too. Cutaz didn't care for Oculis's arguments against telling Elisia so much, he was a foolish dragon.

She was thinking all this while walking around in the garden; bringing to life the poor burnt grass and fixing the statues Cutaz had broken. A sudden glimmer of a sword found its way to her eyes; she stopped thinking and turned towards Argent.

He was looking at the gate, she saw his intentions straight away, he was going to leave.

"Why?" She echoed into his mind, "Why leave Elisia? Hasn't she had enough pain in her life?"

He put his sword back in his belt, and stared at the gate again. Oculis turned to go get someone to help her persuade him not to leave, but she needn't bother. Cutaz arrived.

"Boy," His voice echoed, "It is nobler to leave, but noble to stay."

Argent looked at the dragon with consideration in his eyes. "How could I possibly stay when I bring trouble with my inheritance? I can't do magic, I'm just a sword bearer. If I didn't have my sword I would die."

Cutaz looked at him with wide eyes, "Perhaps, but magic is a part of you. You just have a different form of magic, Argent."

Oculis felt Argent's brain whirling, he was deciding what to do.

"Your magic is tied to your emotions, happy or sad, angry or confused; you receive assistance from the greatest part of you."

Cutaz flew off, leaving Argent to turn around and head back into the house.

"Foolish dragon?" She heard her thoughts echo.

*****

Evening had fallen and Elisia was sitting cross legged on her bed, looking at the spiritual book she had found on the top shelves. Tenebrae had warned her that it was never wise to play with death, but she wasn't playing. She had respect for the book, and it knew that.

Her knowledge of magical books had grown, if the book was too powerful for your eyes it would not open or let you touch it. This book had let her open it, but on the first page it's inky swirls had made her swear to respect the book and it's magic, or she would not be allowed to use it again. It made her realise that magical books (in a sense) did indeed have the souls Cutaz had told her about.

The page she was looking at was probably the only spell in the whole thing that interested her. It was entitled "The Legend of Calling."

By reading the information on the page, Elisia had begun to realise how powerful this spell was. If she alone could master it, she could call Gratis's spirit to her and let it deliver her a message, and then it would go.

Obviously, she had confirmed this with Cutaz before heading up to her room to try it. He seemed to have much knowledge of Gratis, and was more than happy to let her try it ... but he had made her let him watch.

So here she was, sitting on her bed with Cutaz above her peering in.

Closing her eyes and breathing slowly, she recited what she'd been memorising for the last hour.

"Umbră fiind, se întoarcă la mine!"

She opened her eyes. Nothing was there.

Cutaz looked down at her, "try again." He suggested.

"umbră fiind, se întoarcă la mine!" She whispered, again with closed eyes.

Nothing.

Argent climbed up the stairs quietly, he could hear Elisia mumbling something in her room, which had woken him. He felt like there was something wrong, and since the dragon had told him his powers worked with his emotions he trusted the sense.

He crept towards her door and listened in, he was in his pyjamas (that's kind of embarrassing) and surely it would be bad of him to go in? Wasn't it rude to enter a ladies chamber? Didn't matter if he thought something was wrong.

So he knocked twice, and when a mumbled, "Come in," was said by Elisia he entered.

How pretty she looked when he saw her.

He coughed as he cast that thought out of his head, "You alright?"

As Elisia peered up he suddenly realised she was crying.

Argent had grown up most of his life with his mother, and he'd never seen her cry. He had no idea what to do. But his instincts seemed to take control and before he knew it, he was sitting on her bed with a concerned look on his face.

"You probably think I'm pathetic." She said smiling, wiping her tears away.

"No," He whispered softly, "I think you're the best damn runner, dancer, witch and person I know. And I won't say that twice, so don't ask me to repeat it."

He looked at her again, and then cast his eyes around the room.

"I just ..." She began, "I just feel like I've got all this power and I don't know how to use it."

Argent nodded as she began going on and on about everything that was bothering her. If he was honest, he wasn't listening. He was thinking of other things.

Eventually, Elisia fell asleep, and Argent pulled the covers over her shoulders, and carefully placed the spell book on the floor. He sat for a while, looking around the room. Wondering who built it and why, his thoughts whirled many possibilities. But these ideas halted as soon as he realised that dawn was upon him, slowly, he got up to leave. Just as he was at the door he heard Cutaz say sleepily "Love is sacred, love is kind, love is the purest feeling you can find."

Argent turned his head and glanced at the dragon, with one hand on the door knob he replied "Shut your mouth."

Elisia faded into her dreams calmly, she knew the Night Child couldn't visit due to the dragon scale, so she was calm.
A scene came before her eyes, a scene of war, dead men, blood and a dark sky. She had never seen anything like it, a witch war was bad, but not as bad as this … she looked around her surroundings, studying for any signs of life within the corpses, but there was none. Elisia turned around and as a cloaked figure stood before her with a hand out, she screamed.

She awoke, at first panicking and looking for the Night Child, but then realising that dream meant something.

How did she know it did? The look on Cutaz's features told her everything she needed to know.

The house was quiet, too quiet.

*****

Elisia was currently up, washed and dressed, and if she was honest she was panicking. Nobody was in their rooms, the only person near her was the great dragon, and even he would not awaken.

She had searched the whole house, the whole entire thing, but nobody was here.

"Think Elisia," She told herself, "Look for things out of place."

Scanning around the room gingerly, she could not find anything out of the ordinary. Eventually, she returned to her room to think, only to find an envelope seated on her pillow.

With caution, she picked it up and opened it.

Dear Child,

We met before, but I no longer have time to play your games. You have the locket, and you will bring it to me on the 11th of May at midnight, in the heart of this forests domain, or suffer the grief of never seeing your lovely little family again.

Marcellus

Elisia put down the note and wanted to cry. In fact, she did cry, she let tears slip from her eyes as she climbed up to the Cutaz and gave him a poke.

He didn't stir.

She did it again, harder.

He didn't stir.

She smacked him this time.

He didn't stir.

Something was wrong.

Elisia was still pondering on how to wake him up when a sudden whisper made her turn around, but nothing was there.

She shook herself and went back to thinking, until she heard it again.

"I must be going mad," she stated.

All the same, the whisper did not stop. Every few minutes it would happen, and Elisia was at loss to try and find the source, until she realised that maybe, just maybe, she should try and listen to the sound.

She listened, but all it did was whisper.

"What do you want!" She whispered at it.

But it carried on whispering what sounded like a spell. Someone, or something, was trying to put a spell on her, she boiled with rage.

165

"*Arată-te!*" As quick as a flash, her vision became altered and she saw a lot of things she could not see before. One of them was Gratis, flying very close to her face. Surprised and shocked, Elisa stumbled back into a book shelf. Catching herself on the frame, two books fell off and crashed onto the floor. Although Gratis was shown, she still could not hear what he was whispering.

"*Vorbeşte mai tare!*" She ordered again.

Gratis suddenly spoke up, and she could hear him saying an incantation, she had been right.

"Why are you trying to curse me!" She shrieked at him, but he said nothing. Instead, the eagle shook its head and pointed up with its wing.

"You want me to curse the dragon?" She yelled again, shocked.

Gratis shook his head, and pointed to his beak and then up.

"Ah." Elisia understood at last, and repeated the incantation on Cutaz. Immediately, the dragon began to stir.

Elisia turned to say thank you to Gratis but he wasn't there.

"What an earth happened?" The dragon questioned down to Elisia, but then he stopped. "I sense a deep trouble within you, young one."

Elisia began picking up the books and putting them back on the shelves, and then she halted, hand still on the last book she placed back.

"You don't know the half of it." She replied.

Cutaz could not believe his ears.

He could not believe what Elisia was telling him so much that he actually cast a spell so he understood the events of what had happened. The girl was telling the truth, and from what the letter had said, she had made an enemy. Perhaps Elisia didn't know how much danger she had just walked into, but he did know that the best solution was to research this enemy. Not go gallivanting after them.

That was Elisia's solution.

"Elisia, I cannot let you do this. You are not being wise."

She continued packing.

"Elisia, please, you are not thinking straight ..."

166

She stopped what she was doing and looked up at Cutaz, tears filled her eyes.

"I have no other choice, I have one day to bring the locket to this man, and then I will get my family back. They are all I have, please listen to me."

Her voice was shaking, she was extremely distressed.

There was a pause.

"Then, I will come with you." He stated.

She shook her head, "you can't leave, you're trapped here. If I could get you out I would, but I don't know how."

The dragon let his mind whirl for a moment, and then he struck an idea.

"The invisible chains that bind me here are strong; Tenebrae chained me up in order to keep me from causing havoc or attacking people. He stated that one day, when I am truly remorseful of my actions, they will break."

Elisia's eyes widened, "what kind of havoc?" she asked.

Cutaz shook his head, "my father was killed by a spy, and in revenge I murdered him and set about destroying thousands of villages. I am not remorseful."

Elisia climbed up to the roof and looked him straight in the eye, "you killed my mother."

Cutaz looked at her in shock, "no, that is not possible, I could not have ..." he trailed off, the sudden realisation hit him.

"But Cutaz, I do not hate you for it ..." she whispered, as a tear slipped out of the dragon's eye. "You acted because you had lost what should not have been taken from you, and for that I am sorry. You can still make amends to me, to everyone. You can help me save my father and my only family!"

Cutaz looked the child straight in the eye, she really was too wise for her age. "I am sorry for my actions."

Cutaz managed to show Elisia a weak smile.

"Now," she said, jumping down onto the bed and beginning to pack again, "let us go kick some bad guy butt."

*****

Cutaz flew with ease through the many clouds and landed with a bump a few yards from the forest's centre, they still had until tomorrow's nightfall by the time he had landed.

"Thank you," Elisia whispered quietly, sitting down on the floor and hugging her knees.

Cutaz spotted this sudden change of character immediately, she had gone from being very confident to very quiet, and he knew why.

"This burden is not your fault, young one." He said softly, "you cannot blame yourself."

She didn't reply.

"Elisia, you are like the night sky." He whispered with a smile.

She turned round and sat back down, "how so?" she said, interested.

Cutaz looked up to the many twinkling stars, almost teasing him to try and grab them knowing they were too far out of his reach. "You are surrounded by darkness when you are a pure light; there is so much of you yet still to be discovered … you seem so little, but you know so much."

Elisia crawled up against a tree and shrugged, rested her head on the roots and tried to sleep, knowing full well she couldn't.

Cutaz looked at the child huddled up to the tree, she was clearly very cold. With a gingerly swish of his tail he picked her up and placed her down within his wings, she didn't object. She was grateful for the warmth and the kind gesture, eventually (despite thinking she wouldn't be able too) she fell asleep.

Cutaz had looked down on her and felt a glow of pride in his heart, he had to admit the child was growing on him.

Chapter Twenty-One

Bruises

Now, Argent was not one for being chained up and forced to go somewhere. In fact, he was not one to be pushed around at all. He had fought with his captors the moment they had seized him, Oculis, Tenebrae and Gemini. He seemed to be the only one plotting a way out.

Of course he was the worst treated, it made sense, he was young, the captors considered him as weak and feeble. The moment he had been shoved in the dark cellar someone had beaten him until he couldn't speak.

Oculis had been treated far better, they had recognised her immediately and never bothered to even chain her up! They just took her with them. In fact, she was probably sleeping in a closed off room, with a bed.

All Argent had was a floor to sleep on.

It wasn't all bad, despite being alone in his cellar he was able to converse with Tenebrae and Gemini through the bars, it was a comfort, being able to speak to someone in such dark times.

"What I don't understand is how they got through that damn gate unnoticed!" Gemini whispered to Argent, "Surely Cutaz would have felt them in some sort of way?"

"He was asleep; they put a spell on him the moment they arrived." Argent replied simply.

This meant his captives were, indeed, highly trained in magic. This would make it hard to escape.

Argent staggered up, and with much objection from his wrists, he broke out of his chains.

This earned a gasp from Gemini, "how the diddle aunt did you do that?"

The sword bearer said nothing, he just felt around for a way out, but there seemed none. Surely places like this have secret tunnels or switches or **something** to help them get out. He started to become desperate, his patience wearing on his fifth trip around feeling the slimy cellar walls.

"Sit down boy," said Tenebrae from somewhere in the cellar to the right of him, "The only way out is the main entrance, and we cannot go that way. I suggest keeping the energy you have, they will return ..."

"To beat me ..." Said Argent stubbornly, wiping his fingers on his jeans.

"I'll make sure they don't."

"How?"

No reply came from Tenebrae; obviously the man had a secret trick up his sleeve.

*****

Oculis was being treated to the highest standard, they feared her, and she was glad to know they did ... for she feared them too.

A mixture of hate and fear had collided in her bones at the sudden realisiation at who exactly was behind everything, and when she came face to face with him, she was glad to see he was slowly withering away.

"You don't look your best." She stated, keeping her face expressionless.

A smirk flickered on the old man's lips, "It's good to finally meet who I'll be going down with if the little rat succeeds in her task." He sat down shakily on his chair.

Oculis suddenly realised his motives, he wanted her to help him take Elisia down, to kill her, to stop her from destroying the locket once and for all.

"It has your soul," He said in a low voice, "when it finally bursts open its power will kill everyone I hate. I am the blood relative of the man who created it, it is entirely in my power."

Oculis raised her eyebrows but did not move at all, her fear made her freeze.

"You will do well to keep on the good side of me, and not steal my locket from my grasp again." He told her, "Because if you do ... if you ..." he coughed, "You will suffer!" He breathed wheezily. "You will help me get it back, without me it will ... kill many innocent people."

Oculis felt the need to point out that with him it would kill many more innocent people, but she kept her mouth shut.

"It is killing you." Is all she said, and to her surprise, the old man smiled.

"Indeed it is ..."

To Oculis's dislike he seemed to have recovered from his coughing fit. "Just goes to show that it is using my energies in the way I intended. It lives with me, my soul and the locket are bound now. Its power will always spring to serve me!" He sighed, "Let me tell you my wonderful well thought plans, you'll be impressed."

"Do you wish to impress me?" She said.

The old man said nothing.

*****

Argent was woken by the sound of someone hurrying down the cellar steps and grabbing the bars of Tenebrae's 'room'. He silently listened to the steps, often people can judge who it is by how they walk.

"Oculis."

She whispered some information to him, and then hurried out.

"What did she say?" Argent asked, walking over to the bars and pressing his head on them. They cooled his skin.

He heard Tenebrae sit on the floor and say "We're going to be used as a trap."

Argent heard Gemini swear under his breath.

Elisia was in danger, and Argent could do nothing. He punched the bars in anger, "No!" He yelled.

*****

Elisia awoke to sounds of horses galloping nearby. Cutaz was already awake and alert; he gave a nod to Elisia, as if telling her everything will be fine.

She immediately got up and began to move towards the heart of the forest, being cautious to take cover. These people were probably armed with bows and arrows, and wands. She couldn't take any chances.

Elisia wished she had someone with her, anyone. The dragon was left behind, he was too big to sneak around like a fox ... she needed something, anything. And as if the nature around her heard, it sprung to life, beginning to move out its branches out of the way. She could have sworn the trees where humming tunes to calm her.

Her nerves still shook violently; if she failed this, if she lost her family ... the thought wasn't even bearable.

"Believe in yourself, Elisia!" She whispered, hoping this would help to grow her confidence ... it didn't.

She went to take a step towards the bare growth that marked the heart of the forest, but at this point the trees would not move for her. In fact, they held her back.

"What are you doing?!" Elisia whispered at them impatiently, "I need to go through there!!"

A voice filled her head quiet suddenly, the dragon was speaking to her through the scale she wore around her neck.

"What is wrong Elisia? I sense your distress and impatience." He echoed into her mind.

"The trees are holding me back! They won't let me through!" She echoed back.

"Remember, a tree's spirit has been alive for thousands of years. It will know much more then you do."

With that, the dragon's voice disappeared from her mind and the tree's loosened their grip. They seemed to be warning her that the place she was stepping was extremely dangerous. Well, she already knew that.

172

She peered round one of the trees, which moved its leaves so she could see but not be seen. She smiled.

By the looks of things, they had Tenebrae, Argent and Gemini all tied on the floor, on their knees with bags on their heads. The sight was almost laughable, until you realised the horror of the situation.

An idea suddenly sprang to her head.

She turned to address the trees to tell them her plan.

*****

Tenebrae was not comfortable sitting on the floor not being able to see, it would be nice if he could at least see Elisia, if she offered the locket and freed them. He hoped she wouldn't.

He was listening for everything, and something seemed much more fidgety than usual; the trees.

Magical trees moved a lot; that was doubtless. But the fact they were literally humming and whispering was suspicious. Their captives seemed to notice this.

"What's happening?"

"Why are they doing that?"

"One of the horses has got loose!"

"But I tied it up!"

"You clearly didn't!"

Angry confused voices began filling the air, they were blaming each other. The trees began creating more havoc, so much so that nobody noticed Tenebrae's ropes being whipped off by a branch. The same branch picked him up and placed him within the cover of the forest.

"One of the prisoners' has gone!"

"This is your entire fault! I told you not to place them like that!"

"How was I meant to know the trees would attack?"

The cloth on his head was pulled off by one of the branches, he mumbled thanks and watched as Argent's ropes were whipped off, and he was dragged off screaming into the cover of the forest.

"Hmm, I never asked him to scream. Has a good effect though." Said a familiar voice behind him.

He smiled at his daughter, "clever girl."

They both returned to watch the show.

Gemini was hoisted up and placed in the cover of the forest gently, next to Elisia and Tenebrae.

"That was brilliant!" He squealed, still caught between laughing and breathing with relief.

Elisia didn't smile back.

"Where's Argent?" She said urgently.

And before anyone or anything could stop her, she ran out on to the bare lands heading for the other side of the forest.

"**Argent!**" She called, running for the other side.

He appeared out from the bushes pulling twigs from his hair, "I think I did quite a performance."

Elisia sighed in relief and came to a standstill.

"It's the girl!"

"Shoot! Shoot!"

She'd forgotten their enemies were still around.

Time slowed, Tenebrae could only watch as a crossbow was aimed at his daughter. He could only yell at her to move as a horrible metal clunk told him it was too late. He began to run, but he couldn't out run an arrow. It whizzed through the air; hitting his only child square in the arm.

Tenebrae saw his daughter look at him in shock; frozen on the spot. Her eyes slowly flickered in and out of staying open or keeping shut; she began to fall back.

He could only run to her aid and hope he caught her before she hit the ground, but she thumped down hard before he could reach her. Her limbs pounding down on the floor, her body suddenly, distressingly still.

"**Dragon! Draaaaagon!**"

Tenebrae looked around to see Cutaz flying towards the men, he seemed to have perfect timing. Fire erupted from his mouth, and all the bodies fell, even after death they still burned. The dragon landed down.

"What happened?" He demanded to know.

174

Argent looked at Elisia's wound, the arrow was imbedded pretty tight but he pulled it out. "It wasn't our fault! She ran out!"

"You should take better care of the ones you care for!" Spat Cutaz, not registering the sword bearer's panic stricken face.

"Calm down, I'm sure she'll be ..." Tenebrae trailed off as he saw Elisia was already building up a layer of sweat on her forehead; her hair was sticking to her head. She was feverish. He lent down to look at the wound and moved Argent gently out of the way, her skin felt clammy. The arrow was poisoned.

Gemini was knelt down the other side of Elisia, clasping her hand with a worried expression on his face.

"Damn. Tenebrae she's really burning up. What do we do?"

Tenebrae didn't know what to say, his tongue felt heavy, but he managed to hide his own concern with an expressionless face. He needed to be strong, for the others at least. Despite this, he still didn't say a thing.

"We shall take her to the Spirit Pools of Alfa." Said Cutaz simply.

Nobody objected, in fact, everyone just stayed silent.

"I cannot take you all there; I would rather just take Elisia by myself."

Tenebrae nodded, "of course, tell her we'll be on our way there. It might be a four to seven day march but we ought to. Try and heal her with magic while you there, and press the water on her wound and forehead. It'll help control the fever and infection."

The dragon nodded and placed Elisia on his back, before he flew off Argent turned to him.

"Do not blame me for this."

The dragon looked at him dead in the eye, "But I blame you entirely. You always have to make an entrance. That is the problem with incompetent people, they do not think, and if they do, it is wrong."

Gemini stepped in at this point, "There's no bloody need to be so rude!"

Cutaz ignored him and flew off, leaving Argent feeling low and guilty.

The silence that hung in the air after Cutaz spread his wings was almost deathly; nobody could bring themselves to break it. They set off with the voiceless thing hung above them all, even an hour later it was still lingering on, but by that time heavy rain had kicked in, filling the atmosphere with some sort of noise, for which Argent was grateful. For a split second, his guilt for Elisia was shoved to the side, until he realised she was up there somewhere wounded and sick, with heavy rain beating down on her.

He shook his head … His vision of her pain reflected in his mind every time he closed his eyes. He fought with himself and shrugged the guilt off with his brutal side. It doesn't matter, it doesn't matter … it doesn't matter …

He chanted it over and over in his head, but still as he pulled himself out of his thoughts he was met by the heavy silence, guilt racked his aching bones again.

Gemini's view on the matter was completely different; he let himself be racked with worry. Despite this, he wouldn't allow a silence to go on. It would shove rocks between the friendship they had took too long to build.

"Is anyone else wounded?"

"No." Replied Tenebrae, and Argent just shook his head. Tenebrae turned on Argent.

"You are hurt. Don't lie. I've seen the bruises."

Gemini came to a standstill, and was silently watching the matter unfold before his eyes.

"It doesn't matter." Argent replied, looking Tenebrae straight in the eye. Gemini praised him for his bravery, he, himself, would not have looked Tenebrae straight in the eye out of fear of the gaze he would get back. Argent then tried to push past Tenebrae and winced as the man seized his shoulder and ripped the shirt back.

Gemini raised his eyebrows in shock.

Argent's arms, back and neck were covered in bruises, cuts and red patches. As Gemini looked more closely, he realised the different between each bruise. The bruises on Argent's arms and neck were finger prints; he'd been held tightly against a wall and smacked with a metal rod.

"What the hell did they do to you in there?" Gemini demanded to know in a low voice.

Argent desperately tried to cover it up with his shirt, "It's nothing! Nothing!"

Tenebrae and Gemini looked at each other in equal concern, but each man had a different mix of emotions along with it. Tenebrae had an angry determined look on his face mixed with his concern, while Gemini had a genuinely caring concern with distress.

Tenebrae sat the boy down under shelter of the tree and began to look at the wounds much more closely, "I saw them before, but I had no idea how hard they had hit you." A flicker of concern passed over the man's face as he touched Argents ribs one at a time, twice Argent winced.

"That's two broken ribs ..." He stated, and looked at the boys knuckles, "and a broken knuckle. You fought back hard."

Gemini breathed, "So he'll recover then?"

Tenebrae looked up at him, concern flashing his face again. "The fact he was dragged off by the trees has made his ribs worse." He turned to look the boy dead in the face, "You are badly injured, you need to be carried or you need to lay down and not move much for at least three days."

Gemini suddenly realised that Argents screaming as he was dragged was probably genuine.

"Carried! Three days?! **No!**" he said crossly, "We have to get to Elisia!"

Tenebrae shook his head, "You're our number one priority at the moment, she'll be fine with the dragon."

Argent laid his head back and moaned in annoyance; at least the boy was resting, thought Gemini.

*****

Oculis struggled to refrain a smile when she heard the news.

They had escaped.

177

Nobody had told her face to face of course, she'd heard Marcellus's shrieks of fury. **"Then get after them! Find them!"**

She pressed her ear closer to the door.

"But sire ... they have a dragon. Both Sir Liance and Sir Limith are dead, along with two others who we are unable to recognise due to their burns ..."

Marcellus was silent for a minute, and then he said "Send for Oculis!"

She quickly bolted into the kitchens and pretended to be looking at what the servants were making her to eat, lovely people they were. She often found herself chatting to them one way or another.

"Lady Oculis?" Said a serving girl who had poked her head round the door, "You are needed in the council chambers."

Oculis sighed, waved goodbye to the servants' and exited into the hallway, from there, she walked in a slow pace and went through the doors with ease, "You needed me?"

Marcellus looked her up and down before saying "Shouldn't you bow before your king?"

Oculis could not contain a laugh, "But you are ruling no lands!"

He frowned at her, "Surely you've heard the news ... no?" He signalled to a guard and mumbled something in his ear, and smiled. Then the guard departed.

There was three taps on the doors a minute later, and they were opened to reveal a guard dragging a witch into the hall.

"Let go of me! Let go of me you ugly brute!"

"Me and this witch have made an agreement." Marcellus said, "When she dies, I'm next in line to her throne. So why wait?"

Kerkavia was shoved onto the floor with force, on her knees and in a low voice, she shakily whispered "But you said you'd spare me."

Oculis looked at him with horror as a smirk appeared on his face.

"I lied." He whispered.

"But ... b ... but!" Kerkavia gulped as tears poured down her face, "you ... you said ..."

Marcellus laughed, "I say a lot of things. Now, let's make this quick. I have a meeting with the next clan witches I've captured."

Oculis was stunned, but anger began shaking her bones. In her mind, her ink sisters warned her not to let her emotions take control, but it was a little too late for that.

Her veins pulsed anger, and as she looked down at her hands her veins were a lot darker than usual. They pumped dark ink blood, and without warning, her eyes began getting darker too. She closed them, but when she opened them again the ink would be dancing there for all to see.

She stepped forward.

Marcellus's breathing quickened when he looked up at her. "**Guards!**" he screamed, "**Guards!**"

Her eyes snapped open.

"**Guaaarrrds!**"

Marcellus cowered back in his chair as she took another step forward.

"Release the witch." She ordered, knowing her voice was much louder and more echoed than usual.

"N ... n ... no!" He whimpered.

She picked up his walking stick and crushed it, by the time she opened her hands again, it was nothing but dust.

"I shall release her for you."

And with ink magic, she created a portal and ordered Kerkavia through it. The witch did as she was told.

As soon as the witch had gone, the portal closed and Oculis was back to her normal self. Shrugging her anger off, she walked out of the room, her footsteps being the only noise within the horrific silence.

*****

Elisia knew where she was, but not how she got there, she knew she couldn't wake up yet, but she didn't know why, she only knew the basics, and she didn't like it.

She constantly weaved in and out of blacking out and almost opening her eyes, sometimes she was able to move a finger and other times she wasn't. She felt so helpless, she couldn't speak, and she knew it had been days since she arrived, days since she had used her voice.

If the young witch was honest, the only thing she wanted to do more than anything was talk. She wanted to complain about the searing pain in her arm until everyone yelled at her for complaining, she wanted to scream in someone's face, whisper the greatest magic. She couldn't even do that.

She dreamt, at least that was a relief, but her dreams were strange. She heard and saw people she hadn't ever seen before, she sensed so much pain and grief, yet so much faith and hope.

Voices filled her head; they had been for ages now. It was always when she was about to give up, about to stop fighting the poison that she would hear them. They called her all at different times in such little whispers, they sang rhymes Elisia had heard before and she couldn't think where, they gave her hope.

What confused Elisia the most about this whole thing were the cold hands she could feel on her wound, they seemed to caress her arms and heal, but yet they scared her. She didn't know what they were.

The darkness engulfed her again.

She twirled in and out of dark dreams, blood and gore splattered them in many different ways, but it was always present, always lingering, always around. She hated it. Within her mind she closed her eyes on these dreams, and when she opened them, they would be gone.

Again, she closed her eyes within her mind as a man before her was about to be shot, she waited for the heart wrenching sound, but it never came.

She opened her eyes within her mind to see a field, a field with golden plants growing slowly and dancing in the cool breeze. Elisia walked forward, she felt comfortable here, like she was at home at long last. Someone appeared in front of her, someone with a red cloak and white dress, the figure lowered it's hood and Elisia recognised her instantly.

"Mother?"

Mirum nodded, and took her daughters hand.

"Elisia, it is not yet your time. You must go back."

Elisia looked around, "Am I not in the cave with the pools and spirits?"

Mirum looked at her daughter and dropped her hand, stroked her hair and stepped on to a path Elisia hadn't noticed before. Elisia followed.

"You are, but part of you is so hurt and injured it is wanting to dwell here."

Elisia looked at her arm, but her mother shook her head. "It is your mind wishing to stay here, you feel like giving up, like you've had enough. But you must keep going, you must! Even in darkness you must hurdle on through! Your destiny awaits you!"

Elisia felt a tear slip out of her eye, "But I am so weak."

Her mother shook her head again, "No, you are strong. You are stronger than anyone, and I am so proud of you Elisia, so proud. Keep me proud, believe you are strong. You are the sword that fights against the other, you are the ringing clash when they cross, you are the wind that leads the fire, and you are the light within the shadows ... do not give up, never give up."

Elisia closed her eyes tight, and when she opened them, she realised she was looking up at a black rock ceiling with running water dripping down the sides, with someone singing a song in her ear:

"With angels to guide her alone, to home. She'll crack open the bellum with skin and bone."

She turned to see who was the source of the soft voice singing the song, but she saw no one. All the turning did was hurt her arm, she grunted.

"Oh, your awake are you? At last."

She recognised Cutaz's voice immediately, and tried to sit up to look at him.

"No, you need to stay down child, that arm is still sore," he ordered.

She fell back on soft leaves, "Sore just isn't the word, Cutaz."

There was a silence, Elisia (personally) was conserving her energy as she felt weaker than a worm, she figured Cutaz just didn't have anything to say. She clenched her teeth as a burning sensation threatened to rip her arm off, she scowled.

"Where am I?" She whispered out loud in a low tone, mostly to herself, but Cutaz overheard.

"You are dwelling in the Spirit Pools of Alfa."

"How long have I been here?" She now fired her questions at Cutaz.

"A week, the others will be here soon. They have sent word to be here in two days."

"What happened?"

There was a silence.

"You do not remember, child?"

There was no mistaking the concern in his voice, she could not remember anything. She cast her mind back and squinted in the darkness, trying to remember something, anything.

"I just remember Argent being dragged off somewhere, and I ran after him ..." she recollected the vague memories that constantly drifted in and out of her head, she could not remember any further then running after him, just darkness.

The dragon looked at her with his big silver eyes, judging whether to be honest or lie. He came to his conclusion as he looked at her confused face, frowning in the darkness. Lying was not going to help the child gather her thoughts, and he knew that.

"You were hit by a poisoned arrow."

She breathed out shakily and felt her arm, it stung at her touch. "How long till I am able to move without pain?" She asked, staring at the ceiling.

"As long as it takes." He replied simply, which meant he didn't know.

182

Chapter Twenty-Two

The Silent Treatment

e lisia's next few nights were terrible, she often fought with sleep as sleep only brings her more and more dreams. Dreams of sight into the unknown, dreams of cloaked figures and sword bearers ... dreams which were not a figment of her dark imagination, to her horror, these dreams were something more than just a blinding engulfing state of fear that she felt within her core now and again. These were much more.

She didn't want it.

But she didn't have a choice.

Cutaz knew what was happening, her magical skills were growing, and soon she would understand exactly what the future could hold before things happened, if she welcomed it with open arms, of course. If not, she would find these things were pressed into her mind forcefully by spirits who needed her to see them...he prayed, for her sake, she would open her mind to them.

He slept.

His dreams were never tortured by Night Childs, they didn't dare go near him, cowardly creatures, ever so cowardly. His dreams were messages from certain beings, and right now there was one being constantly visiting him; Gratis.

Cutaz was flying over pure white mountains, covered with deep snow. The sky was clouded with grey, but he didn't mind, he knew that despite the cold and grey, it was a beautiful landscape.

He landed down on a platform shadowed from the winds by the mountains, where an eagle darker then the night sky was awaiting his arrival.

"Elisia is not healing correctly."

Cutaz didn't say anything to the eagle, he had many, many questions, but he would not ask them. This was the dark creature who almost killed off Elisia.

"You must see to it she gets better."

Cutaz still did not speak a word.

"I will take your silence as a clue that you are listening. Make sure you say the correct spells, it's of rather high importance."

With that, Gratis flew off. Leaving Cutaz to wake up, feeling a little annoyed with the bird's ignorance to his silent treatment. Did he not feel it?

He didn't care, clearly. All he cares for is the child ... Cutaz looked over to the child who was moaning and desperately flickering her eyes to awaken, he whispered an ancient prayer for her sake, and she stopped fussing, slowly she smiled.

"Sleep now," He whispered at her, "Do not fight it."

Elisia just kept smiling.

*****

The dark night crawled over Argent's sore bones and skin, he was entirely alone. Night was when Tenebrae and Gemini went hunting, of course, Tenebrae was always the one to bring back the meat, Gemini was the one who was always empty handed.

His eyes were open, he was laying on the floor, breathing heavily although he knew he should not. If he made his lungs expand too much, his broken ribs would pierce them, and not even magic would be able to save him then.

He slowed his breathing and made it lighter.

The fire crackled to the right of him, he was under strict orders not to move a muscle until Tenebrae and Gemini returned. He wanted to sleep, but he knew he could not.

He allowed his mind to whirl through many different possibilities and ideas that meant nothing to him, suddenly, he stumbled upon a question he couldn't escape.

Where was Oculis now?

*****

Oculis was packing, quickly. She had to escape, it was only a matter of time before they strung her in a cellar for what she had done, she needed to move, to get away from here, from danger.

Her bag sorted, she slung it on her back and took a look at herself in the mirror, the red dress she was wearing did suit her, her hair was down, it would be less suspicious if she left with her dress on. People would think she was just going for a walk, hopefully.

Speeding down the stairs she was met by a maid.

"Lady Oculis, are you leaving?"

Oculis nodded, the maid could be trusted. The maid leaned closer to Oculis and revealed earth eyes, green with brown and a hint of golden light. Oculis had never seen such eyes before, and was puzzled by the uniqueness of them. Eyes were the windows into the soul, and earthy colours, and even golden light in itself, meant much power and greatness within the witch who possessed them.

"I will cause a diversion so you can leave safely. I know our paths will cross again, my lady."

She looked at the maid and felt a trusting sense within her, and nodded. She went down to rest of the stairs hurriedly and was met by no guards, whatever diversion that maid had done, it was big.

Whispering a prayer for the maid, Oculis slipped away into the night, finally away from danger.

*****

Elisia's eyes snapped open.

"Cutaz!" She clenched her teeth as she struggled to get up, "Cutaz! It's Oculis."

The dragon opened his eyes reluctantly, what an earth was the child rambling on about now? "What about Oculis, child?" Cutaz said, with a bored tone of voice.

"She's ..." Elisia breathed heavily and went on speaking, "She's alive, but she's in danger. Please Cutaz ..."

Suddenly twigging the child's idea, he shook his head.

"No, I will not."

"You ... will!"

Cutaz used his tail to try to ease her back, even in weakness, she still fought his decisions. He respected her for this, but not enough to change his mind.

"I will not, and that is final."

She grunted with pain, "Then ... then she will surely ... surely die!" She coughed viciously, and fell back. "I need ... I need you to ... go."

"This is the last fight of the poison, if you pass this, you will make a full recovery. I cannot leave."

She fell silent. He watched as she fell into a deep, uncontrollable sleep. He whispered a prayer for Oculis; which was heard.

*****

Morning brings light, and for that Argent was grateful. He'd made it through the night and by Tenebrae's calculations they were one hour away from Elisia, as well as treatment for him, and for that he was grateful. He was a very grateful sword bearer.

Although, right now, lifting his sword required effort he did not have, and he knew he could not stumble on for much longer. He just hoped he could keep his legs moving until they got there, then he could collapse. He hoped no one would notice.

Gemini noticed. "I think we need to rest." He said in a soft voice, nudging Tenebrae to look at Argent.

"No, it's fine." Argent stubbornly replied, casting Gemini the death look.

Tenebrae turned round, "I don't want to stop, so ..." Tenebrae cleared his throat and put his pointed his hand at Argent, "*fugere!*"

Argent felt his legs lifting off the floor, "What the ..."

Tenebrae silenced him, "If you hover, then you're fine. I'll control you. Just relax."

Argent found it difficult to relax mid-air, but he didn't kick up a fuss. That would only slow them down. They needed to get to Elisia as quickly as possible; whatever it takes.

*****

Elisia paced the spirit pools, still trying to sense for Oculis. She threw down the rock she was holding in frustration.

"Nothing is working!" She yelled furiously, her echo sped around the room then came back to her ears. As if telling her it really wasn't working, and nothing would.

Cutaz had been ignoring her for some time, taking no notice of her angry voice despite hearing it clearly. He rolled his eyes at her, tired of her pointless spells. If Oculis is to die, then so be it.

"How can you be like this?" She yelled at Cutaz, "Who do you think you are!"

He didn't reply.

"**You're meant to be a** ..." She stopped mid rant, suddenly still.

Rustling was coming from outside.

She carefully stepped towards the door, picking up a stick as she went. It wouldn't be much use, but least it was something.

Closer it came.

"**Declare yourself. I'm armed,**" She ordered in what she hoped was a threatening voice.

"With a stick?" Cutaz hissed at her mockingly, she shot him an angry look.

"Elisia! It's Tenebrae, Gemini and Argent!"

She recognised the voice even before he'd said their names. She ran out, open armed and engulfing her father in a hug. He stood there, not returning it. To her confusion one of his arms was up, as if he was controlling a spell. She followed where it was pointing and saw Argent, awkwardly waving at her from above ground.

"What …" She questioned Gemini, but he just shook his head and pulled her out of the way as Tenebrae went past guiding Argent into the cave.

"I think I need to catch you up on what's happened, and in return you tell me how your recovery went." He said, turning to walk down into the forest of Alfa.

She followed him, "Why is Argent unable to walk?"

He heard the concern in her voice and smiled, "He'll be fine. He just was a bit mistreated when we were bloody captives."

She frowned, "Don't sugar coat this. What happened?"

He sighed as he was walking, "He was beaten, a lot. I won't go into details because I have a delicate stomach," He rubbed it and made a face, "but it was bad. He's got two broken ribs and a broken knuckle, Tenebrae says he fought back hard …" He shook his head sombrely, "Anyway, what happened to you?"

"It's a really long story." She said, picking a leaf off a nearby tree and began ripping it into pieces.

"You'd better hurry up and tell it before it gets dark."

She smiled. The pieces of leaf twisted and danced as they fell to the mossy ground beneath her feet, staring at them, she took a deep breath and began.

Chapter Twenty-Three

The Wounded

Alfa was a beautiful place, and after days of staying here Elisia was sad to leave, but she had a mission, and that mission must be completed.

She sat with the group, laughed at jokes, and when all fell silent, she voiced her decision.

"I'm going to go to Annikia."

Silence.

Tenebrae did not look at her, Gemini was looking at her in amazement, Cutaz was smiling in amusement and frankly she could not tell what Argent was feeling.

"Why?" Inquired Cutaz, a smirk pasted on his face.

"I am going because it is right at the edge of our world, and nearest to here. I have to go, cast the locket out."

She cast her eyes at Argent, she caught his eye. For a second, they looked at each other, he in shock, she in guilt.

"It is in war!" Burst out Tenebrae, standing up and sending his bowl clattering to the ground. Elisia's eyes tore from Argent and looked upon her fuming father; he stood staring at her, letting his words burst from his lips. "You will die! And if you do not die, you will see wounded men and women and it will poison your mind! You will not go."

His face fumed a cold fury which only showed Elisia that he had made up his mind, but she had made up her own.

"I'm aware."

Another deathly silence.

"You will not go, and that is the end of the matter." He said stubbornly, and turned to pick up his bowl.

"I am, and you will not stop me."

He spun around, marched over to his daughter and slowly crouched down to her height and looked her straight in the eye, "You dare disobey me?"

"Yes." She whispered, staring back into his eyes.

To her bewilderment, she was not seeing the same cold fury that was on his face, instead, she was seeing a deeply frightened man within his eyes. He clasped her arm, it was only then did she realise he was shaking.

But is it from fear ... or is it from anger?

"Disobey me and I will disown you."

She raised her eyebrows at him, fearless. His weakness was her strength, and right now, she needed as much of it as possible. "You wouldn't."

He kept on staring, and for a second a spark of confusion flashed his face, as if wondering how his daughter knew his secrets, but soon it was back to the same cold fury to hide the frightened man.

"I would."

With that, he got up and went outside the cave. Leaving Elisia to deal with the awkward glances she got from Gemini and Argent, and the cheeky smile of amusement on Cutaz face.

As night fell she moved quickly, weaving in and out of the sleeping people. She froze, staring at the tired eyes of her friend and made another swift decision.

Elisia crouched low, and carefully nudged him.

"Argent?" She whispered, nudging him again.

He moaned quietly in annoyance, and opened his eyes at her.

Elisia hadn't really noticed the colour of his eyes before, they were a dark blue; she looked at them for a moment, finally noticing that his soul contained much sorrow.

"Elisia? Where are yo …" He faded off as Elisia made a few desperate hand gestures for him to stop talking.

She pulled him up and grabbed his bag, put it on his back then marched out of the cave. "You're coming with me!"

He looked up at the moon and felt his ribs, it would do.

"When did you decide this?" He said, walking on through the forest.

"A few seconds ago …" She hurried after him and smiled, "And no," She said, "No you don't have a choice."

She saw him shrug from the corner of her eye and smiled again, at least she was not alone.

"So," Elisia said, moving under a branch and holding it for Argent politely. "How are your ribs?"

Argent swiftly moved past her with a smile said, "Fine."

"Good."

Silence.

"Why is this so awkward all of a sudden?"

Thoughts paced through Elisia's head, ever since they had left the camp, awkwardness had become between them. She felt like she'd just met someone and she was being polite just because she didn't know what to make of them yet.

"Did I say something?"

Argent hadn't seemed to have noticed the silence, at least, he wasn't giving anything away.

"Where are we?"

"I don't know."

She turned on him, and stopped him in this tracks.

"What is the matter with you?"

He stood stone faced and staring at her, meeting her gaze.

"Nothing."

She held her gaze and realised something had changed. Within his soul, she saw more sorrow than usual, more frustration, and more restraint. She knew he wouldn't own up to it, not even if she used magic. There were some things you couldn't even force people to admit, no matter what.

"What's the point of having him here if all he's going to do is be a miserable brat?"

"Go back." She ordered, turning on her heel and heading away from him.

He followed her.

"Go Back!" She yelled in his face, pointing to the edge of the valley.

He made no turn, he just looked at her, stared at her.

"You're a miserable brat."

"Friendly." He replied.

Elisia was usually a calm, collected person. She never got angry, never flipped out, never lost control of her body.

This time she did.

Her fist curled up and made a full blown contact with his face, fist against flesh collided in force, sending him backwards on to the floor with thump.

He didn't move.

"Argent!"

She ran forwards in a panic.

"Shi …" She faded out as he opened his eyes and stared at her.

Silence held them both in disbelief.

"You hit me." He whispered.

Elisia looked at him grimly, lost in shame at what she had done. "I … I didn't think. It wasn't my fault … I … I …"

Argent stared at her.

"I … I'm sorry."

His hand found its way to his face; it softly caressed the area and winced as he touched it. He staggered up and away from her; lost in shock and fear.

"You hit me!"

She shakily got off her knees and lifted herself up, "I know … I'm sorry. You just made me angry and I couldn't control it." Her hands were up in surrender, she wanted everything calm.

Argent's eyes blazed in anger, "You still hit me!" he yelled at her viciously.

"Then come hit me! Will that make you feel better?" She yelled back frustrated, anger blazing in her eyes now. It flashed on her face and made her shake, it boiled her skin. She felt it, pure white hot anger pulsing under her flesh.

His hands went down by his sides and he conjured his sword.

"An eye for an eye, a tooth for a tooth." He spat, running forwards with it raised in the air. His expression determined, his eyes locked on his target.

Her scream echoed for miles.

*****

Oculis sat down inside the cave, with Cutaz and Tenebrae, not believing her ears.

Part of her was proud of Elisia, the young witch was doing the right thing ... but part of her was disappointed and concerned for her, setting out on your own was never a good idea.

"Do you know if Argent went with her?"

Tenebrae looked clueless at Oculis in reply, it was Cutaz who used words.

"It is my guess that Elisia woke him up and took him with her."

Tenebrae got up and put both hands on the cave walls, as if attempting to push it over. "Why wouldn't she take me?"

A laugh erupted from Cutaz, "You?" he spluttered, "You told her she could not go! If you had not said anything about banning her from going on her travels, she, and we, would not be in this mess."

Silence fell between those three.

"Where's Gemini?" Oculis voiced.

They both looked at her and shrugged, this time, it would seem, both clueless.

*****

A cloaked figure on a horse moved fast through the trees, alerted by the scream of a girl. The horse galloped heavily, but no sound came through. It was as if the horse was as light as air.

Its rider pulled on the reins hard and the horse stopped obediently as its rider dismounted, and then it trotted off into the trees, carefree.

The figure moved silently, and stopped isolated in the cover of the shadows.

It watched as a young man felt the pulse of a girl, and yelled in frustration. But then he fell silent, and just gazed out into the darkness, not seeing the figure.

It sighed and began whispering a prayer, which was heard immediately.

But there must be a punishment.

The figure watched as the young man suddenly fell back, clutching his mind and screaming loudly. It didn't look away, not until the final scream had been heard as dawn was rising.

A whistle made the horse appear and the figure mounted and galloped off into the faded light of a new day.

Chapter Twenty-Four

How Did You Survive?

A rgent breathed heavily in disbelief at himself, also in shame.

Guilt.

He'd never felt such a strong, pulsating vibe of guilt within him; he'd never felt such a strong desire to change what he'd done. He felt it, as the realisation suddenly loomed over him that he could not change what he had done, nobody, except perhaps a being of extreme magic, could.

He thought it was over.

He sat up, head still whirling, and looked at the still body of his ... friend. No, to him she was more than a friend, she was family.

He desperately shuffled over to her, and turned her head; praying that the mark of the Devil's Eye was not there.

It was.

He screamed loudly in frustration, and took out his sword, wanting to kill himself through the devils eye.

"Let me change it! Let me take her place!"

Another wash of guilt crashed over him.

He screamed again, in pain.

He fell back on to the damp ground clutching his head; he felt as if the life was being drained out of him slowly. He shook himself; suddenly realising Elisia was stirring.

"Elisia?"

He yanked his life back; she stopped moving.

"Elisia? Are you there?"

Argent sat still for a moment.

Then, he let his life go.

He opened his eyes.

The first thing he noticed was a graceful, black cloaked figure standing before him, the slender hood moving slowly in the breeze. He then looked around him, he was not on his earth.

"Argentum." A woman's voice erupted from the cloak; although loud, he found it calming; pure ... he wanted to hear it speak over and over again. It echoed in his ears, it seemed to swim around his brain and stop his blood from flowing angrily fast. He was suddenly comfortable.

He looked where the face should be, but could only see shadows. The cloak hood was too low.

"Who are you?"

"Someone ..." She replied.

Argent moved away from her, despite not wanting too. "I don't have time for this, I'm looking for Elisia."

The figure seized his arm hard, refusing to budge.

"You will listen, Argentum, you will listen."

He stopped and peered at the cloaked figure's hand.

It was pale, pale like parchment, like the moon had shone upon it for hours. Soft skin and perfect natural nails which were not too long. He found himself stunned, and part of him seemed to sense she, the witch, was different from anyone else he had met.

So, he used his ears, and shut his mouth.

"You," She said, "You are much more then you seem. You hurt Elisia."

He gulped in worry, "Are you her mother?"

"No." The witch replied quickly, "I am not."

"Are you any relation?"

"No."

"Then why do you care what I do to Elisia?" He spat angrily, "You are no Selphina, and you are no Goddess!"

196

He regretted saying that the moment it came out of his mouth.

"Calm yourself, or you will hurt."

"Is that a threat?"

"No, it is what will happen."

He fell silent as she walked him into a deep layer of woodland, he walked round a fallen tree.

"Do you not see the beauty? The purity within this one branch?"

He raised an eyebrow in confusion and humour, "was this woman mental?"

She seized him again and made him look.

"You have forced me to use force. Look! Look how the branches twist together as if they have frozen within dance, listen to me. Nature is beautiful."

He mumbled a small reply under his breath.

"Come, you must hear me."

She walked forward into a clear cut field and stood facing away from him, still and alone, then the cloaked woman suddenly turned to him.

"There is much to think about. Elisia, and her father, maybe even Oculis. But for now, we must just look at what you have done; what the consequences are of your actions."

He suddenly realised, to his extreme pleasure and yet dislike, she was going to visit him more than just the once.

She gestured him over to her and made him sit down, and then continued to gaze onwards into the distance.

"Elisia is alive right now, breathing ... but only because you gave your life to her. You shouldn't have. She was meant to die, see me, and come back."

Irritated, Argent said "I'm sorry for messing with the fate of Elisia" rather sarcastically.

She ignored him, "Point is, you need to go back. Elisia will stay alive but she will be weak."

He clenched his jaw, "Right, anything else?"

"You will be punished for this; greatly."

"Fine."

He closed his eyes, lost within the plight he was in currently; and when he finally felt prepared to open his eyes and face the world, he was looking at up at bright blue sky, which seemed to be greying fast.

Argent laid still for a moment while his soul returned to him. At first, he was confused at what had happened but after a while he began to realise that he was back within his own little world.

He felt smaller than this world, much smaller. He lay realising how fragile life was, and how easy it can be ripped away. Maybe it was just the journey of almost being dead that shocked him, maybe it was how much he was shaking now, but all the same he was suddenly afraid of all things evil … that included the sword he carried himself.

Shakily and slowly, he moved his strong stomach muscles and sat up. Out the corner of his blurred eyes he saw her, and he turned to get a better view; her eyes were open and she was staring at him. He tried not to look at the expression on her face.

She whispered at him in disbelief, "You."

"Wait, I know I did wrong but I have to tell you something."

"You! You tried to kill me! You tried to kill me!" She screamed madly at him, up on her feet now, but shaking. Shaking a lot, as if standing up on her own was hard.

"I know, but I gave my life to you and …"

She interrupted him, "Shouldn't you be dead?"

"Yes! But …" He shouted at her, but she shouted over him. "You're dead to me! I'll get you!"

He took a step closer to her, "Look, calm down!"

"Get away from me!"

And then, despite her weakness, she backed away from him, screaming at him. He felt her pain, he felt her fear. He felt his own fear at how scared she was, he tried to tell himself she was over reacting but somehow he knew she wasn't. Deep inside, he felt someone ripping at him. Each piercing scream caused him pain; each hurt would cause him hurt.

She whimpered and ran, ran limping into the dark, unmerciful forest which would pray on limping little girls.

"Elisia!"

He only called her name once, but by then she was gone. He fell to his knees, overweighed with guilt, fear and depression. He couldn't close his eyes; he saw her scared face every time he did ... her scarred neck.

What had he done?

"Argentum ..." Whispered the wind, "This was your punishment, I am truly sorry."

Such a heavy price to pay, such a heavy price indeed.

*****

Tenebrae sat alone, staring into the cave walls blankly. His thoughts were gone; they'd left with Elisia when she snuck out into the cold air of night. His heart was too broken to feel; he didn't know what was going on anymore.

"You are not well in the mind, Tenebrae."

The dragon's voice echoed around the cave. Tenebrae hardly had noticed it was just him and Cutaz, in fact, he'd hardly noticed anything after having another person ripped away from him by fate.

"Elisia is not dead."

To Tenebrae, those words didn't matter. She wasn't where he could reach her, she wasn't within his protection.

He replied lowly, "She is as good as dead."

Cutaz growled, "You are wrapped in your own thoughts. You cannot see the bigger picture. You are ill in your mind; you are depressed."

"I don't get depressed."

Cutaz growled at him again, "Let me show you what your child is doing right now."

The dragon muttered a spell under his breath, and immediately a swirling pool of bright light shot up from one of the pools of water on the floor, and hung in the air where Tenebrae was gazing so intently.

Tenebrae fell back in shock, scrambling up he cursed Cutaz to the fire breath of a Benistron.

199

"Just look you incompetent ill thing."

He was just about to spit a few nasty words of his own when he suddenly saw Elisia in the swirling pool of light; she was limping, her face showed pain every time she tried to move forward.

She was struggling.

Tenebrae gazed on for a moment, hardly aware of his thoughts moving swiftly back, whirling together into one. He hardly noticed the numbness flooding away. Most of all, he hardly noticed the bright spark of wanting to protect her begin to light into a fire inside him, he grabbed his bag and slung it over his shoulder.

"She needs me."

Cutaz nodded in agreement.

"Off you go."

So Tenebrae left, running like when he was a little boy to a rescue mission of some far off princess. He used to climb trees and swing down them, apart from when he got the end of his mission there was nobody there, just a few pieces of a broken imagination. He could never imagine the princess waiting for him, not even if he'd tried.

This time, he prayed that there would be his real little one waiting for him.

Chapter Twenty-Five

The Site

She'd spotted it.

She sat gazing, a searing pain was all over her body but she still managed to focus her eyes on just what she was seeing.

It was a camp, a camp that was preparing for war. Wands were held by all personnel and broomsticks were propped up against the enchanted walls which seemed to hide them if someone walked near, it didn't seem to matter who they were. Tents were placed all over the place, and after every three there was a camp fire. Spies, trained assassins', and witches sat themselves near the fires warming themselves; this was usually after broomstick training or an eight mile run. Elisia had noticed that they almost never sat by the fire after combat training, they always seemed too hot and avoided them and went towards the nearby lake instead.

She felt someone poke her.

"Tell me who you are or I'll rip your spinal cord out and use it to play *The Sailors Tune*."

A male voice, a very low male voice.

Elisia found she couldn't speak.

"I can hear it now. Pluck, pluck, pluck pluck, da dum, **pluck**." He carried on humming in Elisia's ear.

"Leave the poor kid alone, you ugly brute."

A woman's voice now joined the picture. If only Elisia could turn round and explain.

"Please," Elisia gasped hoarsely, "I can hardly move, I mean no harm!"

She felt someone kneel down beside her; slowly they placed their hands on her shoulders and turned her towards them.

Elisia saw a witch who had past the prime of her age; her face seemed to have hardened from war. She looked strict, but in her eyes Elisia saw compassion, sympathy ... a loving magical being who shouldn't have seen what she has, but she did. The witch had dark brown hair which was tightly pinned back, with a red war beret placed on her head at a slight angle. She was in a black war uniform, something only the army wear.

"Oh Ictus, look how pale she is. I can feel her pain from here!"

Elisia guessed Ictus was the male.

"She looks fine to me, Misericordia."

Elisia also guessed this was the female.

Misericordia's face suddenly turned dead cold, she stared at the man, "Pick her up and bring her back with us ... plus, you will call me Lieutenant M. Cordia, I might be your sister but that doesn't mean you can back chat me, Ictus."

"Yes ma'am."

Elisia felt herself be hoisted up by a strong pair of arms; this helped her get a clear view of Ictus's face.

He seemed young, at the prime of his age. His hair was red but extremely short. His eyes were dark and his face, like his sisters, was hardened from war. In his eyes Elisia saw much frustration, but strength and power seemed to keep this just below the surface.

"Hello." Elisia said to him, peering up at his face.

He looked at the young girl in his arms and didn't look happy to be carrying her. "Shut your mouth."

"Aye, aye sir." was Elisia's reply to this.

She stayed quiet the rest of the time, just grateful he was carrying her.

202

Soon though, they reached the camp, and were met by a whole crowd of saluting people.

"Lieutenant M. Cordia!" They all echoed loudly at the same time.

"We have found a child, and you will take her to my room and supply her with water, food and wake her at six am tomorrow morning and bring her to me, is that clear?" Her voice was loud and full of authority and power, something Elisia hadn't seen before.

Nobody answered.

"**I said**, is that **clear**?"

"Yes M. Cordia!"

They dispersed in different directions, all doing different things on M. Cordia's instruction.

Elisia was carried into one of the tents and placed down on a bed, within minutes, people brought in food and water for her. Her bag was then removed and placed by her side, and then they left. Nobody entered after that; Elisia was on her own.

She looked around her, grateful for a tent and protection, and … silence. With that final feeling of safety, she fell fast asleep.

*****

Being shaken awake was not to Elisia's taste, but soon she realised that having a loud trumpet to wake her was much worse. She moaned and reluctantly got up and out of the bed she had slept in.

No sooner then she had put her aching feet on solid ground and slung her bag on her arm did two soldiers' walk in, both male, grab her arms and practically drag her through to another tent neighbouring the one Elisia was just in.

M. Cordia sat on a lone table covered with food, one chair spare stood beside it.

Elisia was told to sit down in it, and, without objection, she did.

All personnel suddenly departed from the tent, leaving Elisia and M. Cordia on their own.

"What is your name?" She questioned,

Elisia considered lying for a moment, but then she decided against it. "Elisia Ivy Crewman."

"Why are you here?"

"Would you like the short version, or the long version?"

M. Cordia took a chicken rib and ripped her teeth into it, grabbing a chunk that filled her whole mouth, "The long one."

So Elisia began her story, about her parents, the legend, Marcellus, Oculis, her father … but she left out Argent. She told M. Cordia everything, from start to finish. She even mentioned her powers, but only briefly. There was a certain air about telling it all, a certain relief that seemed to lift everything that had been bothering her off her shoulders.

When she had finished telling her story, there was a silence from within the tent. M. Cordia was staring at Elisia, in shock and in sympathy.

"I am speechless, child." Was her reply to the story, she said nothing else.

Elisia stared on, waiting for a better reply. She didn't just gabble on for half an hour about her life story for a response which contained four pointless, unexplained words.

M. Cordia seemed to realise this, and carried on speaking,

"You have suffered greatly, you seem to be strong, yet I sense a disparity within you. I understand privacy Elisia, but if you need to tell anyone about anything, count on me."

Elisia smiled.

"Now, have you given any thought on what to do?"

"Yes, I wish to go to battle with you."

The lieutenant laughed, thinking Elisia was joking.

"No really, I am serious." Elisia assured, "I have a mission to complete … I have to do it."

M. Cordia looked on at the child sitting in front of her, aware that it was not a child sitting in front of her. It was a fully grown witch.

"Let me think about it." M. Cordia said, "For now, have fun exploring the camp."

Then she got up, leaving Elisia on her own with her thoughts which seemed to whirl over the idea of going to battle.

Elisia realised that if M. Cordia said yes, she would probably join the ruthless training, but if M. Cordia said no, she had so much more to lose then just her life. She would lose all that she aimed for.

Getting up, she headed out of the camp, she was no longer hungry and she was no longer thirsty, she'd taken care of that. However, now she was hungry to explore, and she had a thirst for learning.

She peered around, looking for Ictus.

She spotted him.

Moving in and out of the people like a snake, she sat down and watched him operate an advanced wand. It clicked and reloaded with magic easily enough (although in war they sometimes nick name magic energy as ammo). For a while, he didn't seem to notice Elisia was watching him, but then he looked up, and gestured her over.

"Hold this." He ordered, with a cheeky smile on his face.
Elisia knew he was playing with her, that he thought she was just another toy he could irritate until breaking point. He thought the moment she took that wand it would shoot a spell she couldn't control and she would, to his amusement, blast backwards into the broomstick wall. Well, Elisia had other ideas.

She took it.

She felt it buzz with excitement in her hand; he smiled at her, waiting for it to go out of control. It did not. Instead, it stayed in her hand and within her complete control. Clearly, this man did not know how powerful she was.

His smile faded.

"You will give it back now." He said, disappointed.

She hummed, "No, I think it likes me."

His face turned cold with fury; he disliked being disobeyed by people, especially a child.

"*Transmutare*," she ordered, pointing at a camp fire rock. Within seconds, it turned into a small dog which instantly went for him and bit his leg. He kicked it away and changed it back to normal.

Elisia could see the confusion on his face.

"Hmm, I might just remove your spine, and play Twinkle, Twinkle Little Witch with it."

She chucked it back to him with a sigh, safe within his hands, he tried to spit in her face; she moved out of the way.

"Were you raised by piglets?"

His fury burst over the surface and she ran, he chased her, shouting and swearing at her. To Elisia's amazement, she outran him; it was just the adrenaline of being scared, but at least she had now something she could annoy him with if he ever tried to cross her again. "No point in starting a battle if you ain't got no ammo." Like one of the soldiers said.

The same solider stopped her and asked her for her name again.

"Elisia," She said, smiling and breathing heavily.

"Oy lads! This little kid Elisia out ran Ictus!"

Disbelieving voices from other soldiers could be heard from other tents.

The solider laughed and slapped Elisia on the back hard, she almost fell over but he stopped her.

"Sorry kid, I forget children are so fragile!"

He walked off, saluting her mockingly. She did the same thing back, she was happy.

After that she returned to her tent and got out the book Cutaz had given her, it was reasonably heavy now. She wanted to ask it a question.

"Um ..." She whispered to it, "Can you show me what has happened in M. Cordia's life?"

The pages suddenly flicked and went to a page of another poem.

Elisia read it and flushed with tears.

She more than ever wished that Argent or Tenebrae, or Oculis or Gemini, or even Cutaz was here with her.

But they were not.

The next few weeks for Elisia were back breaking work, just like she'd thought. M. Cordia said yes and ordered her to train hard. Although she was given more breaks then they were because of her aching bones.

Elisia constantly felt tired; every time her head hit that pillow she fell into a deep sleep that, when awakened suddenly, would take a minute before allowing Elisia to wake up.

The only thing she hated (other than the others not being with her) was the trumpet that went off each morning. Although Elisia was allowed a lay in on weekends, it was pointless. It woke her up every time.

She was supplied with new clothes each day; they were often dresses a witch had made or an army uniform that had shrunk. She never got the hat though, despite asking for one from M. Cordia the witch had just laughed in her face.

Elisia had made her way to the lake the day after she had arrived, it was a beautiful thing. Lovely and cool, it sparkled in the sunlight and seemed to play with the droplets of water in the rain. She often found herself near it, reading or not, watching or thinking; it was a peaceful place.

Ictus had been avoiding her most of the time, but she often found him by the lake too. He seemed to be lost in deep thought.

Only once Elisia had gone over to him and asked him if he was alright, he'd said "I'm fine, you stupid child."

She had to ignore this comment.

She often found people calling her a child, this irritated her immensely. Once or twice she'd caught her tongue before yelling at M. Cordia for calling her that three times in the same sentence.

Everyone called her it.

All the time her bones still ached, all the time. She kept asking herself why it hadn't gone away yet, but deep down she knew why. It was something she had driven herself not to think of; right until the point she could hide from it no more.

The locket.

True, Elisia had it in her bag and it was probably draining her energy.

She'd only figured this out three days ago, but luckily she was going to battle in two days.

Forty-eight hours till she lives or dies; if the locket doesn't kill her first.

*****

Tenebrae had walked for miles.

He was used to it; his feet had hardened from his trained assassin training and war. He cast his mind back to the time that he had walked so far that he couldn't feel his feet and laughed. Back then, he'd thought it was a curse, not being able to feel his feet and he'd made the mistake of voicing this to a friend when the Sergeant in charge of the whole operation was within ear shot. Tenebrae had been yelled in the face and forced to walk and extra ten miles for his complaints.

He wasn't someone to complain about life anymore.

In fact, his non-complaining ways has stretched so far that if anyone else is to complain within his ear shot they get yelled in the face; he hadn't made someone walk ten miles for their complaints … yet.

Despite this, he still sat down and nursed his feet in a nearby stream, but only after checking no Water Women lurked within its shallow depths.

None appeared.

So he kicked off his boots and socks and plunged his bare feet into the cold, shallow water, letting out a sigh of complete and utter relief. He stayed there for a while.

Only until he saw the sun begin to disappear, and turn blue, did he stay thinking of the beautiful place.

A blue sun only reminded him of Mirum to much.

After quickly sliding on his socks and boots, he seized his bag and ran into the forest to re-examine the trail he had lost. Elisia seemed to have just disappeared, got picked up by a force and carried off.

That was until he saw the foot prints, with no signs of a struggle from Elisia.

"We're off to see the wizard ..." Tenebrae sang in a tuneless way following the trail. He had no idea he was heading for the place he had escaped four years ago.

Chapter Twenty-Six

Turn off the Lights & Hide in the Dark

$\mathcal{E}$lisia was halfway through her day when a loud trumpet sounded and everyone suddenly grabbed wands and weapons, clicked and loaded them. She'd stood there, confused and panicked when a tap on her shoulder made her turn.

M. Cordia ordered her to go in the tent, turn off any lights and hide in the dark.

Elisia had asked her what will happen if they find her, but no reply had come out of M. Cordia's mouth.

In minutes, Elisia was hidden in the darkness of her tent.

However, there was one thing she couldn't get to stop shining.

The locket was causing her trouble again.

Elisia hadn't noticed it before, but it let out a dim, controllable light which seemed to brighten like hell in the dark.

"Frick!" was Elisia's initial reaction to this, swear words became her reaction after a while. She whispered them while sitting on wet ground in the dark, praying in her head that the light would just stop.

Someone put their hand over the light in the dark, and the hand didn't belong to Elisia.

Elisia shook, she whimpered, she cried, she asked them to leave, she became angry, she kicked them, but no matter what she did they would not go.

"**Get out!**" Elisia furiously whispered, her voice shaking from anger more than fear now.

"I'm not evil, Elisia."

"Then you'll identify yourself." She ordered for the fifth time.

The figure didn't say anything, but a ripping sound could suddenly be heard.

Elisia clenched her fists, expecting the pull on her neck any second now ... but it never came.

Instead, a dark material was wrapped over the locket and thrust in Elisia's hands, and then they departed from the tent. Elisia looked at the locket that could no longer shine; it clearly did not have the power to create a bright enough light enough to penetrate the dark material. She held it in her hands and waited for M. Cordia to come back in, and the Lieutenant did, after two hours.

"We're leaving tonight instead for battle, they just tried to kill us all off before it. It's an act of war."

"They just tried to kill you all! I didn't hear anything!"

"Then you must be deaf."

M. Cordia left after that, leaving Elisia on her own in the dark wishing she really could hide.

She got up and left the tent and shared her thoughts with the solider that had almost shoved her over with a slap on the back, she learnt that his name was Robur and he was 'the man with the meat' in the group.

He looked at her sitting at the table in complete sympathy, "Well, maybe you could just run. I mean, there is that saying "you can run but you can't hide" which is true, you could always run if you're scared in war."

Elisia sighed, he didn't understand. "I suppose; thanks." She got up and went to explore the camp, which actually was big. Elisia hadn't realised there was a whole other area fenced off in the camp, which she jumped over with ease, wondering why it was fenced off.

Her boots hit a blood covered floor.

Cow slaughter.

She wailed in disgust and walked towards the horses in the field, they seemed to ignore her because she was just a "child". Elisia clenched her jaw in irritation and came nearer the horses, being careful to dodge their back ends. Horses have been known to kick people, no matter what age they are.

She was just about to pet one when the trumpet sounded.

It was time to fight.

*****

Elisia had never seen a war field before; she found herself imagining what it would be like. The things she imagined mostly were to do with blood and gore, dead bodies and advanced wands.

As she left the camp entrance behind M. Cordia and Ictus, she began to realise just how much weaponry they had to take with them. Robur seemed to be carrying the most, with six bags full of advanced wands on his back and, he was walking; not using a horse.

Elisia found herself wanting to carry something; she'd tried to pick up a single bag of advanced wands back at the camp, but had found she couldn't lift it off the ground. She also wanted to walk; they had placed her on a horse, mumbling something about "slowing them down".

She didn't like feeling so useless.

Carefully, she reminded herself that she was important. If she had been wrote down in books and documents for years even before her birth, she was important, she was.

They'd only been travelling a few minutes when M. Cordia suddenly stopped, the witches in the sky drew their bows and arrows, the people on the ground took their wands out and loaded them, and the person leading Elisia's horse halted the horse and stood still.

Out of nowhere, a man jumped out and seized M. Cordia from behind. A knife was pressed to her neck.

Ictus was having none of it.

He swiftly caught the man's arm and twisted it back so the knife fell to the wet ground, he then continued to place the man in a head lock. M. Cordia looked furious.

The man looked around him, and Elisia saw his face.

She couldn't believe her eyes, "Tenebrae?!" she hoarsely said, dismounting.

"Leave him Ictus!" barked M. Cordia, clearly remembering who Tenebrae was from Elisia's story.

Elisia did not hug her father.

She stood out of his reach, shocked, and tired of being chased and followed by him.

"Why are you here?"

"I've come," He paused and rubbed his neck, scowling at Icuts, "I've come to help you."

The lieutenant was not amused, "You'll have to walk."

He nodded.

"And, you'll have to carry something."

He nodded again.

She smiled, "Good." then placed Elisia back on her horse, took one bag that Robur was carrying and placed it on Tenebrae. She must have expected him to fall over, but he did not.

"Tell me your name again?" She questioned in confusion.

"Tenebrae."

She hummed, and then went back to walking and leading her army. Everyone moved to follow her, including Tenebrae.

Chapter Twenty-Seven

War

The silent thousand stood facing their approaching enemies.

Nobody moved, nobody spoke; it was a silence to cure those out of control laughing moments, but it was a silence to break your soul into thousands of pieces.

Not even the trees moved.

Even the clouds avoided the grounds; plain blue sky loomed down on everyone.

There wasn't even any mist.

Elisia breathed heavily, looking at all the people surrounding her. She looked back at her father, who caught her eye.

They stared at each other, she in fear, and he in support. His eyes softened, and for the first time ever, he smiled at her.

She did not smile back.

Her cloak breezed against her horse; she had a straight back, and one goal.

She had to get rid of the locket.

The thing was beating in her hand, tapping against its wooden cadge. It wanted to be free.

Elisia looked up as M. Cordia began talking to her people on a broomstick high above everyone.

"We fight today for one goal, peace. They wish to take our land, and it is **our** duty to protect that land with **our** lives. So that is what we will do. Some of you will not make it home …

Some of you will be injured.

But as long as you charge with me, here, now, into the fiery breath of hell itself I will proudly call you my brothers, and my sisters!"

A roar of agreement echoed its way through the crowd.

M. Cordia readied herself.

Elisia took the reins.

Tenebrae held his breath.

Argent took his sword in his hands.

The trumpets were pressed up against their lips, they took a deep, fulfilling breath, and breathed out into the instruments. The sound beat down on Elisia's ears, and she seized her reins and made her horse gallop forward.

She left Tenebrae behind.

Elisia could hear nothing but the sound of thundering people and the shouts of anger and determination, it came from all around. It battled with Elisia's own senses until she felt numb.

The enemy was advancing towards them.

"Just don't die until you've got the locket over the edge," she said to herself.

Elisia breathed and galloped on, she had no sword; just a piece of jewellery in her hand.

Clashes and shouts began to fill her ears; as well as screaming.

The danger loomed closer; fast.

She closed her eyes, the shouts got louder, the screams threatened to pop her ear drums, and the clangs came from right in front of her.

She snapped her eyes open as a determined enemy witch smiled as she saw Elisia, a child, on a horse.

Her sword cut into the horse's neck like a knife into water. In its last breath, the horse veered up and kicked the witch with its two front legs. Elisia screamed as she slipped of its back on to the wet floor.

The horse dropped down right in front of her face.

Elisia screamed again.

She scrambled up and ran through the people, desperately looking for the way out, the edge. Her breathing quickened, her heart pounded, her mind was blank for a minute as she finally saw a way out.

She ran for it, her arms reaching out.

Everything slowed.

A sword from a nearby enemy swung ground; its blade caught her forehead and swooped down to her cheek. She closed her eyes as the pain sunk in.

Anger bubbled with the pain.

She turned her injured face towards them and yelled "*cădea!*"

The assassin fell back into the floor screaming.

Elisia sped up, running for the edge again.

She felt blood pouring down her face; luckily her eye was not damaged, but she was bleeding heavily. She felt faint.

She came into the clearing.

That's when she saw him running towards her, his sword loosely by his side, his arms moving fast against his body. He was looking right at her; his gaze would not fall.

She screamed his name and ran towards him; he slowed down near her, and put a hand on her shoulder.

"Throw the locket now!"

Elisia smiled.

He smiled back.

She took the locket out of her hands and went towards the edge of the world.

Darkness swirled below her.

She extended her arm back, made it whirl forwards and then halted. The locket was held tightly in her hands.

"Elisia?" He said, moving closer.

"Give me your sword."

He looked up in confusion, "Why?"

"Trust me."

He handed it over with no further questions.

The young witch placed the locket down on the ground, and held the Devil's Revenge high over it. She then plunged the blade down into the locket.

Evil against evil smashed together, dark against dark, depression and madness against anger and malevolence; they beat each other until they were both shards of glass.

The Devil's Revenge smashed into pieces and the Bellum Locket broke open.

Screams, screams of darkness, hate, anger but more of all desperate screams broke from the locket. They tore at Elisia's soul, they ripped at her ears and violently bashed against her heart.

Even childrens' screams broke out.

Argent covered his ears and was screaming at Elisia to throw the locket.

Elisia did not cover her ears.

The blood dried on her face as she sat staring, gazing into the locket; she was caught on the screams, caught on the power of the object that could fit into her hands, that was made from nothing but grass and wood.

Nature's bounty …

He watched as the sword bearer touched Elisia's shoulder and yelled something in her ear, he watched as Elisia picked up the broken locket and cast it over the edge.

The screams ceased to exist immediately, but the yells of battle still went on.

*****

He knew what was coming.

He desperately ran closer, screaming his child's name; his only child, the only thing left in this world that keeps him going.

She clawed for the edge but was roughly dragged away; Argent was confused, worried.

"What the hell is going on?"

Elisia clawed for the edge again.

"Elisia! Don't move!"

"For heaven's sake child, please don't."

She reached for the edge and swung her arm up, fist against flesh collided again, madness against anger.

The sword bearer fell back, his body thumped against the floor like a fallen hero.

All was lost.

Tenebrae's lifeline scrambled up; he wouldn't be close enough to grab her. He screamed her name, he ran as fast as his feet would let him.

She dived off the edge with a silent cry.

His life ripped away from his body; another hero, fallen.

Argent clawed for the edge and let go; he fell down into the swirling darkness Elisia had fallen into.

"I'll follow you into the dark."

She'll crack open the bellum with skin and bone.